Nicholas Monsarrat was bor
of a distinguished surgeon. H
then at Trinity College, Cambridge, where he studied law. He gave up law to earn a meagre living as a freelance journalist while he began writing novels. His first novel to receive significant attention was *This is the Schoolroom* (1939). It is a largely autobiographical 'coming of age' novel dealing with the end of college life, the 'Hungry Thirties', and the Spanish Civil War.

During World War Two he served in the Royal Navy in corvettes in the North Atlantic. These experiences were used in his best-known novel, *The Cruel Sea* (1951) and made into a film starring Jack Hawkins.

In 1946, he became a director of the UK Information Service, first in Johannesburg, then in Ottawa. Other well-known novels include *The Kapillan of Malta, The Tribe That Lost Its Head,* and its sequel, *Richer Than All His Tribe,* and *The Story of Esther Costello.*

He died in August 1979 as he was writing the second part of his intended three-volume novel on seafaring life from Napoleonic times to the present, *The Master Mariner.*

BY THE SAME AUTHOR
ALL PUBLISHED BY HOUSE OF STRATUS

HMS Marlborough Will Enter Harbour
Life is a Four-Letter Word
The Master Mariner
The Nylon Pirates
The Pillow Fight
Richer Than All His Tribe
Smith and Jones
Something to Hide
The Story of Esther Costello
This is the Schoolroom
The Time Before This
The Tribe That Lost its Head
The White Rajah

Nicholas
Monsarrat

A FAIR DAY'S WORK

First published in 1964 by Cassell & Company Ltd.

This edition published in 2000 by House of Stratus, an imprint of Stratus Holdings plc, 24c Old Burlington Street, London, W1X 1RL. UK.

www.houseofstratus.com

Typeset, printed and bound by House of Stratus.

A catalogue record for this book is available from the British Library.

ISBN 1-84232-146-3

Cover design: Jason Cox
Cover image: AKG London

CHAPTER ONE

The Man on Board

❖

The view through the porthole was not encouraging. On a rainy day, Liverpool Docks were never at their best; on this rainy day, with the stuff coming down in sheets, spouting and sluicing off grimy warehouse roofs, then turning grimy itself and lying about in filthy pools and puddles on the whole length of Liverpool Landing Stage – on this rainy day, Liverpool looked its depressing worst.

The oldish man staring through the porthole thought: It'll be a grand place to get out of. That was the only encouraging thing about Liverpool, on the dank, dreary afternoon of sailing day. And even that much was uncertain; no one could say whether this *was* to be sailing day, or just another day like yesterday – full of arguments and rows and bad temper, ending in postponement, a dead loss all round.

The man shrugged his shoulders, thin and stooping under the white mess jacket, and turned round to look at the cabin instead. The contrast was enough to bring a brief wintry smile to a grey face cut on grim North Country lines. The cabin – Suite A34 on the passenger list – was immaculate, bright, and neat, and clean as a pin; when Tom

Renshaw moved something, as he did now, setting a bowl of flowers back six inches nearer the mirror, it was just for the sake of moving it. Suite A34 had been ready for the Chairman of the line these past twenty-four hours; and 'ready' meant perfect, in both their dictionaries.

Old Tom Renshaw might not be the youngest, spryest cabin steward on board the *Good Hope*. In fact he was the oldest. But he was still the best.

As he stood back and looked at the flowers, he was listening to the tell-tale footsteps outside the cabin. From long habit, he knew them all; and now they indicated that the passengers were beginning to come on board, from the local hotels where they had spent the last frustrating twenty-four hours at the company's expense. It seemed to Tom Renshaw that they were not stepping lively, as they usually did, but hesitantly, as if they were afraid of being disappointed again. Many of them would be starting the voyage either nervous, or angry, or fed up. That was not going to make the next few days any easier.

Delay was bound to mean worry, cancelled appointments, trains missed at New York or Montreal, sore hearts; it could mean money, and money was always short … The baggage trolleys rumbled past along the corridors, the wheels clicking as they crossed the steel edges of each floor section. A light, hurrying step was a stewardess, already intent on cherishing one of her passengers. Running footsteps were children, excited and out of hand at the prospect of the voyage. The first queasy roll in open water would take care of *them* … A heavy, booted tread was the Master-at-Arms, making his mid-afternoon rounds. Quick tapping heels were probably a girl who was going to enjoy the trip anyway; delay or not, sore heart or not, she would find her guaranteed date with love, under the wheeling boat-deck stars … And the low-keyed knock on the door was almost certainly Suite A34's stewardess, Mrs Webber.

It was. She peered round the doorway, and then came forward; a dumpy, motherly figure, starched of dress, warm of heart and hand. The two of them were old friends, because for thirty plodding years they had found in each other the same things; dependability, a good day's work, a helping hand, no nonsense. Since the Chairman of the line was travelling alone, Mrs Webber would not have much to do with A34 on this trip. But she would give a hand with the bed-making, and clearing up after parties, and answering the bell when Tom Renshaw was off-duty. She would do all these things willingly, and be ready for more, because she and Tom Renshaw were two of a kind.

Maybe it was a vanishing kind. Maybe it was out of date, like the smart young chaps said. But there were still a few left on board the *Good Hope*; enough to share pride in a good job, and disdain for a sloppy one.

Now she came farther into the cabin, and glanced round it with a brisk professional eye, though she knew she could never fault what she saw. The flowers were beautifully done; the telegrams and messages were set out neatly on the desk; the mirrors gleamed, the glossy yellow-wood panelling showed not a single fingermark; the small bar was arranged just as his Lordship liked, with one bottle each of whisky, Plymouth gin, Canadian rye, French and Italian vermouth, chilled Evian water; with an ice bucket piled high, a bowl of maraschino cherries, and a miniature flask of pale baby onions ... She said: 'Now then, Uncle Tom' – the Lancashire greeting which reads like a caution and sounds like a friendly pat on the back; then she went on: 'It looks a treat ... His Nibs not here yet?'

Old Tom Renshaw shook his head. 'No. They say the boat train's going to be an hour late. I don't wonder, with all this chopping and changing ... Did they send up the anchovy toast?'

Mrs Webber nodded. 'I put it in the grill. Horrid stuff, I always say.'

'He likes it ... Has Vic been round this way today?'

'I just chased him out of the pantry. His place is in the Tourist. I told him as much.' Her mouth grew suddenly grim, and she sniffed her disapproval. 'Victor Winston Swann ... He may be your nephew, Uncle Tom, but he's been nought but trouble lately. Always arguing and stirring things up ... He'll finish up in jail, you mark my words!'

'You can't go to jail for talking,' said Tom Renshaw, without too much conviction.

'You can go to jail for troublemaking,' answered Mrs Webber tartly, 'and that's the road he's walking.'

Tom Renshaw sighed, but he held his tongue. He could never really have defended Vic Swann, even though the lad was his own sister's child, because he did not believe, for one moment, that Vic's ideas were worth a penny piece. Between himself and Vic, like all the other young stewards of today, was a ditch so wide and deep that they could scarcely hear each other even when they shouted across it.

Tom Renshaw, sixty-two years old and ready for retirement, prided himself on doing a day's full work for a day's full pay; it was the way he had been brought up, and the way he had chosen, all his life. He had been a staunch union man in the past, and he still was; but all those battles had been won, against cruel odds which had now faded to nothing. Jobs were now reasonably secure, wages guaranteed, working conditions safeguarded by a hundred finicking regulations. There was no call nowadays to talk about the victimization of the working class; it didn't exist any more. Especially, there was no call to walk off the job every time you were asked to work five minutes overtime, cleaning up the mess after a gala dinner.

It was this workshy attitude which he could never share with the young chaps. In his heart he despised them all. They talked of hardship, and they had never known it. They talked of the dignity of labour, when they had never done a willing day's work in their lives. With them, it was simply a matter of what you could get away with; it meant drawing the maximum money for the minimum work. And to Tom's public embarrassment and his private shame, it was his own nephew, Victor Winston Swann, who led the younger gang on board in this shiftless, discontented quest for soft jobs and hard cash.

Old Tom Renshaw was still the senior shop steward, and the official union spokesman, in the *Good Hope*; but behind the scenes Vic Swann did most of the talking, and he had the ear of the younger lot. There was no mistaking that. And one of these days he was going to prove it.

Tom Renshaw sighed again. Times changed, virtues went out of fashion. Sometimes he thought he would never catch up with either. In a shifting world, it seemed that he had been left far behind. Nowadays, 'service' was supposed to be a disgrace; stewards were 'paid lackeys' – they betrayed the working-class movement by 'slaving' for the privileged rich. What a lot of moonshine it was! Yet that sort of talk was persuasive; it made a lot of converts. Already, coming to a disgruntled head in the Electrical Union walkout of yesterday, it had held up the *Good Hope's* sailing for twenty-four full hours. And there might be a lot more, and a lot worse, to come.

He was startled to hear Mrs Webber echoing these thoughts, when she asked: 'Do you reckon we'll get away today, Uncle Tom?'

He took refuge in a question of his own. 'Why ever not?'

'There's been plenty of talk.' She was watching his face, aware of his worries, his behind-the-scenes tussles with people like Victor Winston Swann. 'They're saying it's the stewards' turn next.'

'What turn? Who says so?'

'It's just what I heard.' But she did not want to be pressed; she had held aloof from all this nonsense, all her working life, and she was not going to be involved in it now. 'You know how people talk. Nought else to do, some of them. I just hope it's not true.'

'We'll be sailing,' said Tom Renshaw manfully. 'And anyone who tries otherwise is due for the sack.'

The door behind Mrs Webber had opened noiselessly, without a knock, without even the murmur of a hinge. She turned in surprise as a man's voice said: 'Who's due for the sack? Let's have a few names.'

It was the Chief Steward, Bryce, and the voice, like the man, was poised uncertainly somewhere between the crispness of authority and the soft soap of comradeship. Not quite an officer, no longer a steward, Chief Steward Bryce straddled uneasily, with a foot in each camp.

He was twenty years younger than Tom Renshaw, thin and tall and somewhat furtive; more of an operator, as he had to be, and less of a man. At the same age, Tom could have graduated to the same job, with the wavy gold braid and the wavier status that went with it; but he had chosen not to – he had 'stayed with the lads', as he had phrased it then, and now the lads, what was left of them, were rising sixty, and still cabin stewards, and all due for their pensions in a year or two at the most.

But once again, Tom Renshaw was not sorry. He still liked his job, as he always had; he liked doing it well; he liked passengers asking for the cabins he looked after, voyage after voyage; and above all he would have hated to be a man like Chief Steward Bryce – part-time steward, part-time snooper, part-time tale-bearer to authority.

He knew well that such a man was necessary, within the intricate hierarchy that made a ship work; but he had never wanted the job, not at any price, and twenty years later he was still glad of his choice.

Chief Steward Bryce sidled forward into the cabin (he always walked as if afraid of treading in something nasty); and as he did so, Mrs Webber simply disappeared. One moment she was there, the next she was not; she had glided out like a ghost at cockcrow. Hope Lines, who were always boasting of the 'unobtrusive service' on board their ships, might well have been startled at this demonstration of it.

Chief Steward Bryce, of course, knew that she had gone. But he did not give it public notice; it was a pattern he was accustomed to; if he remarked on it, he might lose what face he had. Instead he stood there, in the centre of the cabin, a tall, stringy, unloved figure, and waited for an answer. Any answer.

'We was just talking,' said Tom Renshaw dismissively, after a pause of his own choice. He did not call the Chief Steward 'sir', and he did not bother overmuch with his tone. He knew Bryce, and Bryce knew him; neither of them had to take any nonsense from the other. Out of this armed neutrality, they both got their money's worth. Thus Bryce, who was the sort of man who normally had to know what everyone was talking about, all the time, now checked this thirst for discovery, and said instead: 'There's a few I could give the sack tomorrow, if I'd a mind to it … I just looked in, Tom. Are you all set up?'

'Aye.'

'The boat train passed Edge Hill,' said Bryce importantly. 'We got a call from the stationmaster. His Lordship will be along in twenty minutes or so.'

Tom Renshaw waited. This was all guff, and they both knew it. After a combined working life of nearly seventy years, neither of them was going to turn faint because the Chairman of Hope Lines was due on board. In this area, things went like clockwork. In fact, better than clockwork. Clockwork could always run down. The *Good Hope*, and ships like her, never did.

Chief Steward Bryce began to come to the point.

'Now all we have to do is get away,' he said. 'We don't want another day like yesterday ... Have you heard anything, Tom?'

'About what?'

Bryce gestured vaguely. 'You know, trouble.' Then he repeated Mrs Webber's phrase. 'There's been a lot of talk, hasn't there?'

'There's always talk.'

'But nothing special?'

'Nought, so far as I know.'

'What about McTeague?' asked Bryce. 'Some of the lads have been slipping ashore and seeing him. I know that much. If I had my way – ' He paused, because – for a hundred reasons reflecting a hundred meagre strands of personality – there was no convincing end to the sentence.

McTeague, thought Tom Renshaw. They were all scared stiff of McTeague, as if they were a warren full of rabbits backing away from a ferret; it was a sort of Liverpool dockside contagion, like the acrid Mersey fog itself. 'I'm not afraid of McTeague,' he said stoutly. 'He doesn't run this union. Nor this ship, either.'

Bryce looked at him. 'So long as you're sure.'

'Of course I'm sure!' Because he was *not* sure, Tom Renshaw's tone had grown almost truculent. 'McTeague's just a talker. Sits in a little office ashore, pulls a few strings, and thinks he's God Almighty. Unofficial union organizer ...' Tom drew a deep breath. 'We expelled him once, from secretary, and we'll do it afresh, if he ever gets his nose in again. And that's a promise.'

'So long as you're sure,' said Bryce once more. 'You know Vic Swann's been seeing him?'

Tom frowned. This was a subject he did not want to open up. 'I'll deal with Vic Swann.'

'Maybe it's high time you did,' said Bryce, with something like spite. 'He's your own flesh and blood, when all's said.'

'Can't help that,' answered Tom Renshaw. 'I didn't father him.' Then, conscious of impropriety – how could he have fathered a child on his own sister? – he sought to get rid of the subject. 'Leave Vic to me,' he said shortly. 'And leave Mr Bloody McTeague to me. I'll sort them both, if I have to.'

'As long as you're sure,' repeated Bryce. It seemed the only crutch he had to lean on. 'We don't want any more trouble with the lads.'

'Leave the lads to me,' said Tom. They were both reproducing set phrases by way of reassurance, and he knew it, and he didn't like it. Needing a rest from this foolishness, he made a firm move to end the interview. 'Well, I must polish up,' he said, not too convincingly. He turned aside, took a napkin from the bar, and began to massage, with intent preoccupation, one of the glasses, his back half turned to the Chief Steward.

It was enough. 'Well, let's hear about it, if anything turns up,' said Bryce. 'You know where to find me.' And he added, on a note of good-fellowship entirely false: 'Do what you can. Eh, Uncle Tom?'

Do what you can ... Alone once more, Tom Renshaw gave up his pretence of work, set back the glass in its position on the bar, and crossed to the porthole again. The rain was clearing, but the skies still lowered; the dockside complexion remained unalterably grey, and pallid, and dreary. From his position at the porthole, he could see the covered gangway, masking the incoming traffic, and a line of slate roofs, and two cranes standing up like abandoned chimneys, and a derrick hoisting cargo and baggage into one of the *Good Hope's* forward hatches. A few groups of men – dockside workers waiting to tend the mooring lines – stood disconsolate, crouching in whatever shelter they could find. Even their cloth caps looked sodden and dispirited.

Whatever happened to the ship, they seemed to say, there'll be no sunshine cruise for us. We'll be spending the rest of the year, maybe the rest of our lives, in Liverpool, in the wet.

Do what you can ... It was what they were always saying to him, in times of crisis. Do what you can, keep things going, patch things up, pretend everything's all right – until next time. Tom Renshaw's eyes sharpened suddenly. One of the reasons why he couldn't do much – why he couldn't do *anything* – was just coming into his line of sight.

Wandering down the quay was a man whom Tom Renshaw would willingly have left behind, along with the rest of the derelicts. He was a young steward, one of the Tourist Class barmen, and he was palpably drunk; he staggered and weaved his way down the length of the ship, his raincoat flapping, his silly moon face shining with the last of the raindrops. He should have been on board, and at work, an hour ago, thought Tom Renshaw grimly; and now here he was, half drunk and wholly useless, and someone else would be doing his job for the rest of the day, and no one would make anything out of it. Even if he were caught at the gangway – and there was no guarantee of that, the slack way it was run these days – he would still be as useless tomorrow.

The worst that would happen to him would be a blast from the Captain, and a ten-shilling fine. He wouldn't be sacked, because sacking didn't work any more. All it meant was that he would be chucked back into the pool, and the union would close ranks round him, with murmurs of 'no victimization', and the first ship out would have to sign him on again – as a steward, conduct average, health good, skill adequate.

It was a process which would continue indefinitely, until he either assaulted a passenger, won a football pool, or missed the gangway and fell into the river. It made a joke out of unions, and a joke out of sailors too.

Maybe that was why they were always saying, do what you can; they knew what sort of trash he had to work with. In the old days, a chap like that young steward – now stumbling his way up the steep slope of the after gangway – would have lasted exactly one voyage; he would have been discharged 'Unsatisfactory' at the end of it, and that would have left a job open for a better man. More important still, during that one voyage his shipmates would have shown him what they thought of a drunken shyster who didn't pull his weight.

But that was the old days, thought Tom Renshaw, when a man did his job and a bit more, bore a hand if a problem came up, and didn't argue about his rights when the time came for an extra effort. Nowadays, the union – all the unions – came down on you like a ton of bricks if you put a foot outside your designated job. Yesterday had certainly proved that.

The quick electrical refit which the *Good Hope* was undergoing should have been finished twenty-four hours earlier. It was just a matter of switching on and connecting up, they said; and though, having watched the electricians at work for five days, Tom Renshaw did not think it would be as easy or as quick as all that, yet it had seemed that they really could not spin out the job beyond sailing time, at 4 p.m. But that was exactly what had happened, and he, Tom Renshaw, had been directly involved in it.

He had come back on board at 6 a.m., after a night at his sister's place outside Liverpool, to find the pantry, and Cabin A34, in darkness. He wanted to get to work right away, in order to have the cabin ready in time, and after a bit of fiddling around he traced the trouble, to a fuse box one deck below. One of the small fuses had blown, cutting out about half a dozen lamps.

It was an easy job to set right, one that any man-of-the-house would do without thinking twice about it; the fuse box was open to anyone, and the spare fuse wire was hanging from a little clip at one side. Yet Tom Renshaw had hesitated, knowing the rules, the silly protective drill which decreed that any electrical job, even replacing a new light bulb, had to go to an electrician, and to no one else. Finally he went in search of the man for the job.

It was no use chancing an argument. There had been too many of them already. But he hoped that it could be put right quickly. He had his own job to do.

It was not put right quickly; in fact, it was not put right at all. He found an electrician – indeed, he found five of them, loafing about in one of the pantries, brewing tea. There was a pack of cards beside the teapot. They had stared at him, in lumpish hostility, as he told them what he wanted; then one of them, a spry, little, argumentative man with a great quiff of yellow hair, like a cock's comb fried in batter, said: 'All right, mate. We'll fix it. Soon as we're ready.'

'I'm ready now,' said Tom Renshaw. 'And I can't work in the dark.' He looked round the company, and they looked back at him. 'I've had my tea,' he said, unwisely. 'I want to get to work.'

'Hark at him!' said another of the electricians. 'Six o'clock in the morning, and he wants to get to work. Take it easy, Dad,' he said cheekily, 'or you won't enjoy your pension.'

The other men laughed. Tom Renshaw stared back at the speaker. 'Aren't you on at six, then?'

'What about it?'

'I'm on at six, too. I want to start my work, and I want that fuse repaired.'

'Now, now,' said the man with the yellow quiff, warningly. His name was Wilby, Tom remembered; there had been a lot of talk about him, the last few days. 'There's no call to take that line. I told you, we'll repair it. Just give us a minute. We're having our tea.'

'On the company's time, eh?'

'What's the matter with the company's time?' asked Wilby belligerently. 'Whose side are you on?'

'I'm not on any side,' said Tom Renshaw, nettled. 'I just want a bit of light to work with, that's all.'

'You'll get it when we're ready,' said Wilby, and lifted his cup, and drank noisily.

'I want it now,' said Tom. 'If you won't fix it up, I'll do it myself.'

There was silence in the little cramped pantry. Finally Wilby said: 'That's electrician's work, mate.'

'What about it?'

'Just leave it alone, that's all.'

'Come and repair it, then,' said Tom. 'It's only a bit of fuse wire. A kid could do it.'

'Is that so?' said the other man. 'Is that a fact? Well, let's just wait till there's a kid ready to do it.'

'I'll do it myself,' said Tom. 'I'm not hanging about for the likes of you to finish your tea.'

He turned to go, and Wilby rose as he did so, in his first show of activity. 'That's electrician's work,' he repeated, on a harsh note. 'Don't you go starting anything. Just you leave it be.'

Tom Renshaw turned back, trying for a last accommodation. 'Are you an electrician, then?'

'The best,' said the other man, and there was a laugh round him.

'Then come and do the fuse.'

'Soon as I'm ready,' said Wilby, and added: 'Your Lordship.'

'When will that be?'

The other man shrugged. 'I told you. When I'm ready.'

Angry at last, Tom Renshaw said: 'All right – I'll do it myself,' and left them.

But he had not left them. They crowded down the corridor after him, the leader and his four mates; they watched him in hard-breathing silence as he put in a new fuse wire, and snapped shut the box. When he turned round again, Wilby said unpleasantly: 'That's electrician's work. I told you twice already. Now you can take that fuse out again.'

'It stays where it is,' said Tom Renshaw stubbornly. He was sick of the whole lot of them. 'I need the light. If you won't repair it, I will.'

'Not while I'm on the job,' said Wilby. His quiff of yellow hair seemed to crest suddenly, like a bantam's. 'You know who I am?'

'No,' said Tom. He was suddenly furious; he knew he was going to be defeated. 'And I don't care. You look like a dog's dinner to me.'

'You'll find out,' said Wilby, on a quick snarl. 'Trying to take our jobs away, that's what you're doing. Don't you know the union rules? Ever heard of the ETU?'

'To hell with the ETU!'

The other man nodded, and they all nodded after him. 'I know your sort,' he said. 'You're with the bosses, that's what. But I'll show you who's the boss here.' He wagged a long, cracked fingernail under Tom Renshaw's nose. 'Are you going to take that fuse out?'

'No,' said Tom. 'And nor are you.'

'I wouldn't touch it,' said Wilby, suddenly cool. 'I wouldn't touch anything round here, and that's a fact ... A slap in the face for the working class, that's what you're trying ... Well, we'll just see who's right and who's wrong.' He turned to his followers, grouped behind him. 'Come on, lads – we're walking off.'

Within ten minutes, there was not an electrician left on board the *Good Hope*. There were hours of interminable negotiation before they consented to come back again. Tom Renshaw had to listen to a lecture – not too serious, but it was a ticking-off, just the same – from the Staff Commander. Meanwhile, awaiting the pleasure of the Electrical Trades Union, the *Good Hope* had to put back her sailing for a full day.

Tom pursed his lips at the memory, and his creased face took on a look of disdain. Changing a bit of fuse wire. That's electrician's work, mate ... He'd like to have shown them how it was in the old days. He'd like to have seen how they faced up to real hardship, real work. He'd like to have told them about the night off the Grand Banks, back in the winter of 1922, when the big wave hit the *Imperial Hope*, putting the steering gear out of action, wrecking the main saloon, carrying away one of the funnels.

He'd like them to have seen how everyone went to work that night, from Chief Officer to page boy; how stewards helped to clear the shambles on deck, and engineers finally tamed the massive furniture sliding from side to side of the saloon, and passengers cleaned up their swamped cabins, and cooks took a turn at lookout duty.

There wasn't any talk of 'That's my job' and 'That's your job', on board the *Imperial Hope* that night. That wasn't the way they had been trained. No one waited for a carpenter to come along and shore up the sagging musicians' gallery that threatened to bring down the whole skylight with it. The man nearest the job jumped to it, and the rest followed him, whether they were stokers or deck hands. That was how it was, in the old days, in times of danger and in times of ease. It had been a matter of pride, a matter of manhood, to believe that a ship was a ship, a job was a job, and only a man could measure up to both.

Tom Renshaw sighed, for remembrance of the past and distrust of the present. Of course those had been hard times, ashore and afloat; and they got worse before they got better. Later on, when ships were laid up by the hundred, and jobs were scarce, a man could walk the streets in hunger and misery, and no one gave him a second look or a second thought. But those things too had passed away. Nowadays, there were no hard times, no scramble for the bare chance to work at any wage, such as he himself had known.

Some battle had been won, some better pattern had taken the place of insecurity and want. A bit of the welfare state had rubbed off on sailors; enough, in fact, to change their whole lives. Looking back over the years, he could be well content with that change. He didn't want more, he wasn't greedy. He wanted things to be the same, holding the level of a quiet, self-respecting life.

But if you talked like that to the young chaps, they thought you were balmy. Or they called you a traitor to your class, or some such nonsense. With them, it was always 'More!' More money, more free time, more food to eat or throw away, more space between trips, more paid holidays; more of this and more of that. Sometimes they reminded him of a nest of young birds, screaming and squawking with open, upturned beaks. And when they didn't get what they screamed for, they turned sulky, they held a protest meeting and walked off the job, leaving work half finished, a ship half ready to sail, and a full black mark against the shipping company involved. Talk about fouling your own nest!

Maybe sailors were only happy at sea; maybe they were not meant to have ties with the greedy life ashore. Today, as on many other days, Tom Renshaw found himself longing for the *Good Hope* to sail – across to New York with her full cargo, down to the Caribbean with a load of cruise passengers. Somehow, this ship *must* get away, and leave behind the infection of the land.

Then, while he still brooded, there came another interruption, in the silence and the waiting of Cabin A34. This time it was the Purser.

Tom Renshaw had a lot of time for the Purser; he thought, in all humility, that he and the Purser shared many of the same ideas, and that they were good ones to share. Now, as the other man came bustling into the cabin – he never walked, he barged in everywhere, and if he barged in on a slack piece of work, so much the worse for the victim – as he came in, the cabin seemed to expand and bulge outwards, to accommodate his lively, roly-poly figure. He moved and talked like a sailor, breezy and cheerful, full of stories, full of comment on everything and anything; but beneath the Jolly Jack Tar manner was, as Tom Renshaw knew, a formidable and even ruthless man.

He was at the top of his profession, and he had got there by working, planning, and occasionally cheating. Of course, thought Tom, all pursers were crooks, more or less; they'd be fools not to be, the way that everyone, from Liverpool ship's chandlers to Las Palmas orange sellers, was ready to give them a cut off the selling price under the counter. But there were two different kinds of crookery. There was the kind that milked the profits and gave nothing in return; and the kind that milked the profits and delivered, by way of squaring the account, a full day's sharply efficient work every time the clock went round twenty-four hours. The Purser of the *Good Hope* was the latter kind; and the ship, and the men in her, got a substantial dividend from the fact, and from him.

Now he came in, rubbing his hands, peering round him with inquisitive jerky movements, like a sparrow the size of an ostrich.

'Well, let's see!' he barked. 'How's Uncle Tom's cabin?'

It was an old joke on board; Tom Renshaw had lost count of the number of times he had heard it, repeated by people to whom it seemed new every time. He did not mind; jokes like that were friendly things, like old slippers always waiting for you, always fitting just right.

'The cabin's on the top line, sir,' he answered. There was no hesitation about the 'sir', where the Purser was concerned; Tom always felt that he deserved it. He added, because it was something that still rankled: 'No thanks to the ETU, either.'

The Purser grinned. 'Caught you on the raw, eh?' He knew all about the Staff Commander's ticking-off; he knew all about everything; the knowledge went with the job – in fact, there would be no real job without it. 'Well, don't you fret yourself. It'll blow over – as the girl said when she left her baby at the top of the cliff.' He rubbed his hands again, more professionally, and his breezy manner sharpened. 'The boat train's in, Tom. His Lordship is just coming along the platform.'

And you want to be here when he arrives, thought Tom Renshaw. But he did not think it spitefully; once again, it was a natural part of the job and of the career. If the Purser always showed his face at the right moments, the face was remembered, when decisions and promotions came to be made. It was as simple as that; it was the way a man 'got on', and one of the reasons why Tom had never 'got on' was because he was no good at it, and didn't want to be.

Tom said: 'Well, we're ready for him ... Many people on the train, sir?'

'Not more than twenty.' It was the kind of thing the Purser knew, automatically. 'Most of them came on yesterday's – we couldn't put them off in time. Today's train was really laid on for his Lordship.'

Tom supposed that this was literally true. Not for Lord Calderstone a shakedown in a local hotel; if there were a delay, he stayed where he was in London, and did a day's work, and caught a later train. And if the train had to be put on specially, Tom Renshaw still approved of the fact. There weren't too many of the old school travelling by ship, these days; it was all rush rush rush by jet plane – fly now and pay never – people seemed to have no time for the proper, the time-honoured way of travelling. When someone like Lord Calderstone chose to go by ship – even if it belonged to his own company, and the shareholders were paying the bill – he deserved the best, and plenty of it.

The Purser looked down at his watch, with a quick gesture. 'Half past two … We should get away by six, with luck. In fact we've got to, to catch the tide over the Bar. I just hope there are no more hold-ups. I had my fill of them yesterday, I can tell you! Sending all those telegrams. Fixing up the hotels. Taking on extra stores. Changing all the dates on the landing cards. Arguments about this and that. I had about enough of it.'

Tom said, without irony: 'It was bad luck on the people that was put off, too.'

'Don't I know it!' agreed the Purser readily. 'There's all their plans and reservations that have to be changed, when they get to the other side. And even if we paid the hotel bills last night, they were bound to need a bit of extra spending money on shore, and spending money doesn't grow on trees. Not any more.' He sighed, not too deeply; these were other people's troubles. 'All I can say is, I hope it doesn't happen again, that's all. For *any* reason.' His eyes flicked sideways towards Tom Renshaw. 'There's been enough people put out, as it is.'

'Oh, we'll get away, all right,' said Tom.

'We'd better.' The Purser now had his head cocked to one side, listening, and Tom Renshaw knew what he was listening for. 'I'm not saying we can't cope with it, because we can, but it's so damned inefficient! There's only two things on God's earth that should delay sailing day; one's a hurricane and the other's a war. Anything else – well, like the girl said to the juggler, it's just a lot of – ' He broke off, suddenly and perhaps fortunately. Then: 'That's him now!' he exclaimed, and stood to one side, looking towards the door.

Steps sounded down the long corridor, quite a number of them; the assorted heavy footfalls of men in authority, treading their own ground. A voice, which Tom Renshaw recognized as belonging to the Chief Passenger Agent, said: 'Down this way, Lord Calderstone. A34.' The great man entered.

The fourth Lord Calderstone had been a household word for so long that he amounted to a brand name; and the man himself, shown in press photographs, seen on television, heard on the radio, or quoted in newspapers, at least once a week in each medium all the year round, was as familiar to the general public as to the faceless insiders of Wall Street or the City of London. Everyone knew what he looked like; a tall, handsome, sixtyish, balding man, strong of jaw, level of gaze, acute of business intellect; a living portrayal of the power and prestige of the managerial world.

He was personable, and spruce; as a young man, he had once been cited as the third best-dressed man in England (after the then Prince of Wales and the second Duke of Westminster); and he still maintained the role of the mature Man of Distinction. But beneath the elegant, mannered façade was a wide-awake human being who could best be described as formidable.

Lord Calderstone had not suddenly happened; no smart deal in South African gold shares, no takeover squeeze in the West End property market, had fathered this man and this image. He was a fourth generation baron who had inherited, developed, and perpetuated the acumen and the toughness of the first generation baron (born 1810) who in turn had made his money, his title and his reputation in North Country iron.

No succeeding Calderstone had ever lost ground. The Lancashire saying, 'Clogs to clogs in three generations', had never looked like threatening this durable family. In fact, it had turned out to be a matter of clogs to buckskin half-boots (by Lobb, of St James') in four generations, and there was, demonstrably, plenty more of the same progress to come. Once having got their teeth into a good thing, the Calderstones had never let go. It was fair to say that they had carried several millions of people with them, on this long road of industrial achievement.

The present Lord Calderstone was still in shipping, cotton, and steel – the traditional North Country money-makers. But he had improved on these staples, as Britain herself had improved. He owned some newspapers – not the really big ones, which he thought of as vulgar and somewhat corrupt – but a respectable string of provincial dailies. He had interests in real estate, and tobacco, and bread, and electronics, and proprietary drugs, and cocoa. He owned, or controlled, a trawler fleet in Hull, a holiday camp in North Wales, a factory which made nearly all the dry batteries in England, and an iron works in Nottinghamshire. He was, inevitably, one of the largest shareholders in commercial television. In *Who's Who,* he listed his recreations as 'Reading and gardening'.

It was his habit, agreeable and virtually unavoidable, to travel in state; and he was beginning to travel in state now, as he entered Suite A34 at the head of a comet tail of supporters. Foremost among them were the Chief Passenger Agent and the Marine Superintendent. There were two other men, in the traditional Liverpool bowler hats, from the Hope Lines head office ashore; there was the Chief Officer and the Staff Commander of the *Good Hope*; there were two secretaries – one, female, carrying a portable dictaphone, the other, male, nursing a large bunch of flowers.

There was a deck steward bearing a massive monogrammed briefcase, and two news photographers in close convoy with a Hope Lines public relations man. Finally, like a diminutive regimental mascot, there came Mrs Webber, holding a silver tray with a covered dish upon it – his Lordship's favourite anchovy toast.

The cabin, in fact, was swiftly full to the bursting point. But Lord Calderstone could hardly be said to be lost in the throng.

He greeted both the Purser and Tom Renshaw by name (among his other gifts, he was tremendously good at names); then he shed his astrakhan-collared top coat into Tom's waiting arms, and sat down at a table in the 'veranda annexe' which formed part of the suite. He looked at the anchovy toast, and exclaimed: 'Ah – you remembered – how kind!' as if it were the nicest thing Mrs Webber or anyone else had ever done. Then he said: 'I think I will have a small – a very small – whisky and water. And see what anyone else wants.'

Tom served them all – and they *all* had small whiskies and water, except the female secretary, who had nothing – before leaving the cabin. Then activity set in. After the standard farewell drinking time of three minutes, the Hope Lines men said their goodbyes, in order of seniority; the

Chief Officer said: 'The Captain's compliments, sir, and he is available at any time,' and also filed out, followed by the Staff Commander. The female secretary unlocked and opened the briefcase, and Lord Calderstone began to look through some papers.

He was photographed four times at this task; once looking up, once looking down, once with a cigar in his mouth, and once tapping his chin with a gold pencil; the photographers were then ushered out by the public relations man, who said: 'Sir, there are only two pressmen. I told them, in fifteen minutes.' Lord Calderstone answered: 'Of course,' and returned to his work.

The male secretary, having disposed of the flowers, leant over the back of his chair and began to murmur and to point out. Presently Lord Calderstone started talking into the dictaphone, and then, after ten minutes or so, switched to the female secretary and began to dictate a series of short, personal memoranda. At the end of fifteen minutes, the public relations man returned, with two newspapermen in tow.

Lord Calderstone had already given a spate of farewell interviews, both at his home the previous day and at Euston Station that morning; this last contingent, unusually small, was merely a minor flourish by way of final goodbye. But he still greeted the two men with the greatest courtesy and charm, as if he had waited for this moment ever since he entered public life; the press had done a lot for him, over the years, and he had done a lot for the press, and he did not intend the relationship to lose its sweetness.

The men were both young – not more than twenty-five. One was from the local daily, the other from that London national newspaper for which Lord Calderstone had the greatest, the most cordial dislike of all. The Liverpool man was thin, hungry-looking, and eager; the London man fat, sloppy, and seemingly half asleep. But one could not have told, from Lord Calderstone's manner, that there was any difference between them. They were both there as honoured guests, and it was his privilege to prove it.

The male secretary having left, and the female withdrawn unobtrusively into a corner, he summoned Tom Renshaw to serve drinks. While this was being done, he chatted easily, not about himself but about his visitors; when the Liverpool man mentioned that they had met before, on a previous sailing day, Lord Calderstone said: 'Oh yes, I remember you well,' and talked about housing development in the suburb of Garston, which was where the newsman lived. Then Tom Renshaw withdrew, after a brief glance round the cabin, and they settled down to the interview.

The Liverpool man asked all the right questions; how many times Lord Calderstone had crossed the Atlantic ('My dear fellow, I lost count years ago!'), whether he was going on the Caribbean cruise after the trip to New York ('Ah, how I wish that I could!'), the prospects for Lancashire textiles (not terribly bright, it seemed, on the whole), what Lord Calderstone had thought of the last budget ('I have never wholly disliked a budget'), and what he was going to do in New York (see friends, talk business) and in Washington (attend a series of tariff talks, to which he was one of the British delegates).

No dust was raised, no mud stirred or slung. It was all as smooth and as innocuous as peanut butter.

The London man played no part, at this stage. He sat there, looking rather bored, sometimes listening, sometimes looking round the cabin with an inquisitive and vaguely unfriendly eye. ('Lounging in his luxurious £500 suite on board the plush liner *Good Hope*, pride of his own shipping empire, Lord Calderstone sipped duty-free whisky, served by his personal steward, and talked sympathetically about the plight of Lancashire cotton spinners.') Lord Calderstone knew the type, and the phrases they used, and the way they angled this sort of interview, and the way they behaved. First they listened, then they tried to pounce on something, turning it over and over in search of the embarrassing item. In his private view, they would be better employed as customs inspectors. But they were, alas, the enormously powerful popular press, and he and the rest of the country had to learn to live with them.

He had trained himself to do so. Thus, when the critical moment arrived, and the needle went in, he was not taken by surprise.

He had been talking about the coming tariff discussions in Washington.

'Of course,' he elaborated, 'it all ties in with the GATT talks later this year.' He paused, and smiled. 'This horrible alphabetical jargon … GATT, as you may know, is the General Agreement on Tariffs and Trade – '

'We do know,' said the London newsman, abruptly. 'But what are the chances of you getting to Washington in the first place?'

Lord Calderstone, ignoring the tone, turned courteously. 'I beg your pardon,' he said. 'I don't quite understand your question.'

'I mean,' said the newsman, 'you're meant to be going to New York, and then on to Washington. This ship is supposed to take you over. Do you think she'll ever get there? In time, I mean?'

Lord Calderstone smiled, though he was not in the least amused. 'Barring an act of God – ' he began.

'I mean,' said the newsman brusquely, 'will she ever get away from here?'

'Why should she not?'

'There's talk of a strike. There's been one already. You were held up yesterday. What about today?'

'That's over and done with, so far as I know.' Lord Calderstone's tone was bland, though he recognized this moment, as any seasoned boardroom warrior would. It was the moment when the spokesman for the dissatisfied shareholders rose at the back of the room and said: 'What about the cut in the dividend? Where's all our money gone? That's what we want to know!' It was the moment which, if not firmly checked, led to fists being shaken, umbrellas waved, and a smooth meeting dissolved into unseemly chaos. He dealt with it now, as he always did to start with, by mounting a polite counter-attack. 'But I may not be entirely up to date. Perhaps you have some information which I have not.'

'I've no information,' said the London newsman rudely. 'That's why I'm here.'

Lord Calderstone, who did not like young men in any case, found this fat and impertinent specimen especially uncongenial. He decided to take a different line.

'Now let me see,' he said thoughtfully. 'What did you say your name was?'

'Barber.'

'Barber ...' Lord Calderstone repeated it, with a wintry smile. His glance did no more than rise to the other man's hair, which was undeniably shaggy. The point was made. 'And your newspaper?'

Barber told him.

'One of the newspapers I do *not* own,' said Lord Calderstone. He and the newspaperman were staring at each other unblinkingly; it was a direct clash, though war had not been explicitly declared. 'But I know its taste for – shall I say? – a somewhat sensational approach to quite ordinary items of news. In this case' – he paused, and gave the smallest perceptible glance towards the secretary, who began to write – 'in this case, I can say that there are at present no indications on board the *Good Hope* of any unrest serious enough to lead to a strike.'

'A real happy ship, eh? Can I quote that?'

'You may quote what I have just said,' answered Lord Calderstone coldly. 'Without embroidery.'

'You mean, she's *not* a happy ship?'

'I did not say, nor imply, anything of the sort. It was your own phrase. You may invent it, if you wish. But you should not attribute it to me.'

'If you're accusing me – '

'I am not accusing you. You said that there was talk of a strike, and you suggested that the ship would be held up again. I have answered that I am not aware of any such situation. I think that disposes of the matter. And now' – he rose – 'if you have no more questions, I have to call on the Captain.'

'Anything special?' asked Barber, undaunted.

'A matter of courtesy,' said Lord Calderstone. 'I do not know if you would consider that as something special.'

The Liverpool man, an embarrassed witness of all this, got up quickly. 'Thank you, sir,' he said. 'Thank you very much. I hope you have a good trip.'

'I am sure that I shall,' said Lord Calderstone.

They were all near the cabin door, in uneasy motion. As he reached the threshold, Barber shot off a last probing spear.

'If there *is* a hold-up,' he insisted, 'what will be your personal attitude?'

Lord Calderstone stared down at him. 'The same as any other passenger's.'

'I mean, angry? Resentful?'

'I do not mean either,' said Lord Calderstone. 'I would be seriously inconvenienced, and I would regret the fact. It would not go farther than that.'

'A lot of people get angry.'

'I am not one of them,' said Lord Calderstone. 'I never get angry. Not even in the most disagreeable circumstances. Good afternoon to you.'

When Suite A34 was empty (like all good stewards, he always knew when any particular cabin was empty, or occupied, or discreetly out of bounds) Tom Renshaw went in to tidy up. He collected glasses, squared up the bar, tipped out the ashtrays, set the chairs to rights, and stepped up the air-conditioning fan to get rid of the smoke. Then, bearing a tray of glasses to be washed, he went back to his pantry, and found himself face to face with a surprise.

His nephew, Victor Winston Swann, was there – though that was nothing out of the way; in spite of their differences, Vic was never backward about dropping in for a smoke, or the loan of a polishing cloth, or a cup of tea when tea was on the brew. But with him was another man; one of the newspaper people Tom Renshaw had just been waiting on; the fat one with the grey raincoat and the dirty nails.

They had been talking when he came into the pantry; Victor Swann was perched up on the counter, lounging back against a cupboard door; the other man was standing below him, twirling his hat on the point of one finger, mumbling through a drooped cigarette. Quick silence fell as Tom Renshaw appeared; then the newsman said abruptly: 'See you later, then,' and Vic Swann answered with a chirpy 'OK, Mr Barber,' and Barber shouldered his way past Tom Renshaw and out of the pantry, without another word or a glance.

Tom was angry, for several reasons. Damn it all, it was *his* pantry ... He set the tray of glasses down, and looked sharply at his nephew.

'Get down off that counter!' he snapped. 'How many times do I have to tell you, pantries are for work, not for lounging about. If you got nothing better to do, give me a hand with these glasses.'

'Keep your shirt on, Uncle Tom.' Vic Swann levered himself down from the counter, at a leisurely pace, and faced Tom Renshaw. 'And I *have* got something better to do, don't fret yourself.'

Tom Renshaw jerked his head backwards, towards the door. 'What did he want with you?'

'We was just talking.'

'I could see that. But what did he mean about meeting you later?'

Vic Swann smirked, and his answer was jaunty. 'I'm going ashore. That's what he meant.'

The smirk and the cheeky tone reflected the man. This was Victor Winston Swann, thought his uncle caustically, as he had thought many times before; Victor Winston Swann, so christened in hero worship and homage in 1942, and bearing this badge of honour ever since. They might as well have called him Hercules ... He was a thin, bony young man, with a mop of curly hair which gave his head its only significance; below the hair, the eyes were inclined to shiftiness, the nose beaky, the mouth pulled into bitterness by a permanent grudge against all better men, all softer jobs, all purer accents, all inclinations to quality.

He had been a nasty bit of work as a kid, Tom Renshaw always remembered; now he was a nasty bit of work grown-up, carrying into manhood every petty instinct of spite, jealousy, and cackling derision which should have been left behind in the schoolroom.

If this was Young England, thought Tom Renshaw, then God help us all! But he only thought it, and said it, privately. For good or ill, Victor Winston Swann was his nephew; blood was thicker, and warmer, than water; his sister's child must be allowed some grudging margin of approval, where otherwise he would have been written off as a proper little bastard.

But he did not have to be given this approval now.

'Going ashore!' repeated Tom Renshaw, in true astonishment. 'What d'you mean, going ashore? It's three o'clock already! We'll be off in a couple of hours. And what about your passengers? You know you've got to settle them in before we sail. You've got a job to do, my lad, and don't forget it.'

Vic Swann blew a smoke ring, making a crude smacking noise with his lips at the same time. 'Who says we're going to sail? I didn't hear about that.'

'Of course we're going to sail!'

Vic Swann cupped his hand to his ear, in vulgar pantomime. 'Must be getting deaf. Tell you what – I'll give them a good wash out tonight.'

Tom Renshaw ignored this, as he had ignored, fifteen years before, Vic Swann spitting over balconies, or peeping through lavatory windows, or chalking 'GEORGE DID LINDA' on neighbours' walls. It was only growing pains, his mother used to say; he misses his dad, just take no notice ... But now the result of missing his dad (which could be true) and growing pains (which was a lot of bunk) and taking no notice (which was a mistake) was with them, a permanent member of the adult world. Tom Renshaw did not understand him, and did not want to. Tom Renshaw was looking for a quiet and orderly life, and people like Victor Winston Swann were well on the way to spoiling his chances of getting it.

As Tom kept a purposeful silence, bending over the glasses in the sink, trying to stand apart from all this nonsense, Vic Swann spoke again.

'What's the passengers matter, any road? A lot of rich folks chucking their weight about ... If I had my way, they'd be waiting on me, and I'd be sitting back smoking a big cigar and chewing away at the smoked salmon … I don't have to settle them in. Let them settle themselves. Give 'em some exercise for a change.'

Tom Renshaw, polishing a glass, said: 'You know very well they're not all rich folks, not by a long chalk. Look at the people you've got in the Tourist. They've maybe scrimped and saved – '

'Then they shouldn't expect to be waited on!' said Vic Swann, reversing his argument without effort. 'Who do they think they are?'

Tom looked across at him. 'Who do you think you are?'

But Vic Swann ignored him. He was well away. 'What's the good of being a steward, any road? Waiting hand and foot on a lot of lah-di-dahs while they have all the fun. Look at old Calderstone, for a start. God Almighty, done up in a fur coat. Never did a straight day's work in his life, I bet! Inherited the lot from his dad! Is that what we're here for? Just tell me that!'

'Just tell you what?'

'Tell me why the privileged classes still get away with a racket like this. The whole class structure – '

Tom Renshaw turned to face him. 'Class structure?' he interrupted. 'Come off it lad! Where'd you pick up a balmy thing like that? And privileged classes? Who are they when they're at home? You talk like some silly young sod on a soapbox. You talk like McTeague!'

Vic Swann reacted quickly to the name; his face took on an alert, almost conspiratorial look. 'What's wrong with McTeague, then?'

Tom Renshaw snorted. 'We can do without his sort, that's all.'

'Let me tell you, it's people like him that's the backbone of the working class.'

'Oh, get on with you!' Tom Renshaw was growing angry; he was ready to argue, in spite of past failures; the glasses in the sink were forgotten. 'Let me tell *you*, the backbone of the working class are the lads who do the work. And McTeague's not one of them. You're not one of them, either. What d'you want to see McTeague for?'

Vic Swann had turned sulky. 'Never you mind.'

'Don't give me any of that sauce,' said Tom Renshaw warmly. 'Else you'll be in trouble.' Then he was struck by a different thought. 'Did that chap from the papers bring a message, then?'

'Who wants to know?'

'Vic! I'm warning you!'

Vic Swann tossed his head. 'I was going to see him, anyway.'

'Just before sailing time? Why?'

'Because we're all fed up, that's why.'

'Fed up with what?'

'Fed up with Bryce, for a start.'

It should have been 'Mr Bryce', and Tom Renshaw was on the verge of telling him so. But he checked himself, wanting to find out as much as he could. 'What's the Chief Steward got to do with this lot?'

Vic Swann paused to light another cigarette from the stub of the old one, and to puff out a wreathing cloud of smoke. Then he said: 'The way he's always ordering us about.'

'That's his job.'

'Not with me, it isn't.'

'What do you want, then?'

'Fair play and better conditions.'

As the pat answer was trotted out, Tom Renshaw expelled a long breath. He must have heard the same phrase, the same bit of jargon, a thousand times before ... They were always talking about better conditions, as if their present conditions were intolerable, as if they were being trodden into the mud by a cruel brute labelled 'The Boss'. It just wasn't true any more, and anyone who had a head instead of a turnip knew for a fact that it wasn't true. Once again, he found himself near to despair. He would never get through to people like Vic Swann.

He would always keep on saying that things weren't so bad, and *they* would always keep saying that they were fed up and wanted a change; the two sides would never meet, even halfway, and the result would always be trouble, silly arguments, ships held up, men left idle ... Didn't they realize they were killing their own jobs, going on this way? Ships were sailing half full anyway, with all the competition and the airlines. Did they want to see them tied up forever?

He tried to put something of this in his tone as he said: 'What's wrong with the conditions? They're a lot better now than they used to be. And the pay's fair enough. If the company could afford more, they'd give it you. But they can't. They're up against it as it is. And you don't need the extra money, either. Not so soon after the last raise. Why don't you give them a chance?'

'They never give me a chance.'

'You won't have a job left, if you go on like this. None of us will.'

'See if I care. It's justice we're after, not jobs.' Vic Swann stubbed out his cigarette, and buttoned his coat. 'Well, I'm off,' he said jauntily. 'I've got work to do, if you haven't.'

'Let's get this straight,' said Tom Renshaw. 'You're going to see McTeague?'

Vic Swann nodded. 'Yeah.'

'To make a complaint?'

'A lot of complaints.'

'Then what?'

'Then we'll see what happens.'

'But McTeague's not an official in the union. Not any more.'

Vic Swann shrugged. 'Who cares about that? People listen to him, just the same.' He smirked. 'People listen to me, believe it or not.'

'I believe it.' Tom Renshaw made something like a last plea. 'But you're on the wrong road, lad. Why not let things be for a bit? Give them a chance to work.'

'Because I don't like them, that's why. I told you, me and the lads, we're fed up.'

'Does that mean a strike, then?'

'I can't promise anything.' Vic Swann had put on the cheeky tone again, but this time he could not hold it; the occasion was too significant. His voice changed to a crafty note – the great and wily leader charting his people's destiny. 'But I wouldn't be surprised. I wouldn't be surprised at all.'

CHAPTER TWO

The Man Ashore

❖

In McTeague's drab dockside office, a meeting was in progress. It was not the sort of meeting which ever reached the minute books; but it was a policy conference none the less. In the great saga of labour's martyrdom, in the bitter struggle for a better world, it counted.

The room was up one flight of stairs over a derelict tobacconist's shop; the flyblown window below, with its grimy paper decorations, was not more forlorn than the office above. It was barely furnished: a deal table covered with oilcloth tacked down by drawing pins, a sofa and two armchairs which had started life as a 'club suite' and were now ending it in shiny, threadbare ruin; an ancient roll-top desk; faded curtains; and a rug worn to shreds on the pathway between the window and the door.

Newspapermen sometimes wrote of this office in piteous terms, as if it were a degrading cross which McTeague the unionized messiah was doomed to bear. But, in fact, McTeague liked the room the way it was; he would not have welcomed the money to improve it. Especially, he relished the idea that from this poor despised retreat he could control the movements of such a barefaced emblem of exploitation as 25,000 tons of gleaming white luxury liner.

He could say 'Stop', and she had to stay alongside; he could say 'Go', and she had gracious leave to depart. Some kind of string seemed to run from this shabby lair to the green and gold Royal Suites on board the *Good Hope* and her sister ships. When he chose to twitch that string, he could make everyone dance. At least, he *used* to be able to do so, and he was going to have a damned good try to make it true again.

So far, the day's proceedings had been informal. McTeague himself was reading a newspaper; the three other men in the room were talking desultorily; at the desk in the darkest corner of the office, a dedicated adenoidal slut was typing out a list of names and addresses. But if the minutes of the meeting had been set out formally, they would have been headed thus:

Present: Mr McTeague (Chairman and Convener)
Mr Wilby (ETU)
Mr Norris (Stewards' Pool)
Mr Barber (Press)
Miss J. Sutton (Recording Secretary)

Presently a voice rose above the clatter of the typewriter, the shrill voice of a man with a grievance. It was Norris, a mournful, bald-headed young man, an ex-steward of the *Good Hope* and of most of the other Hope Line ships; and he had a point to make.

'They had no call to victimize me!' he declared. It was a favourite phrase, hollow with use; a dull parrot, sitting on his shoulder, would have been word-perfect by now. 'It's just plain victimization! You can't get past that. There's not a Chief Steward in the whole line hasn't got it in for me now!'

'You played it wrong,' said Wilby. He was lounging against the mantelpiece; the quiff of yellow hair, reflected in a cracked mirror behind him, was especially prominent today. 'I'm not saying they haven't got a down on you, because it's obvious they have. But you played it wrong, just the same, the last time. Giving a bit of a back-answer is one thing, taking food is another. They've got a case. There's no doubt of that.'

'I was hungry,' said Norris. His sad face took on an extra measure of misery. 'You'd be hungry too, if you had to live on what they give you on the *Good Hope*. Some hope, that's what I call her!'

Barber, the London newspaperman, turned his chubby face towards Norris, with a first show of interest. 'Is the *Good Hope* food bad, then? I mean, have there been a lot of complaints?'

'It's slops, that's what it is,' declared Norris. 'Out and out slops. You wouldn't give it to a dog. Half the lads can't eat it.'

'What do you do when you can't eat it?'

'You state a complaint, that's what you do. And a fat lot of use *that* is. Ever tried making love to a mermaid? . . Well, you state a complaint, anyway. Say it's a plate of stew, like. You don't care for the look of it – it's full of bits of fancy meat and I don't know what all. Chief Steward comes along, and you tell him it's not fit to eat. He picks up a spoon and takes a little taste. Not too much, mind you, or he might throw it all up right there in the canteen. Then he smacks his lips, and looks you in the eye like the born liar he is, and he says: "Delicious! just like mother used to make!" and that's the end of that. You could have saved your breath to cool your tea.'

'Has it ever made anybody ill?' asked Barber. 'The food, I mean?'

'Well, not so much *ill*. But a lot of the lads feel poorly after meals. They'd rather go hungry.' Norris' voice rose again. 'Not me! I'm not going to go short, just because the company wants to feed us on leftovers. That's why I swiped the biscuits and cheese. I was ready to drop! I was plain starving!'

'What sort of cheese was it?' asked Barber, whose editor had a lust for small detail.

'Stilton,' said Norris. 'I like a bit of Stilton. But they keep it for the nobs.'

Wilby, a silent listener thus far, shook his head. 'You made a mistake, all the same. Knocking off the passengers' food – it sounds bad. It *looks* bad, written out. They've got a case.'

'D'you expect me to die of starvation,' said Norris, on a high whine, 'because I can't eat the regular food? Of course I swipe a bit here and there. All the lads do. Sometimes it's a matter of life and death!'

'Well, you shouldn't get caught at it, that's all.'

'Well, I did get caught,' said Norris aggrievedly, as if it were Wilby who had caught him and turned him in. 'And Captain put me off the ship, just like all the other bastards did. Now I haven't worked for six weeks.' He half turned, towards McTeague, though he did not speak directly to him. 'What's the union going to do about it? That's what I want to know.'

McTeague put down his paper promptly. 'Don't fret,' he said, as if he were answering a straight question. 'I'll get you a ship. And that's a promise.'

He said it with confidence, and he looked as if he meant it, and could do something about it. McTeague was always like that; it was how he had made his way in the world. He applied to the smallest individual problem all the skill, passion, and ruthless cunning of a lifetime of struggle.

McTeague was fifty-two. He had kept his hair, which was bushy and iron-grey; he had kept his compact, trim body, an unlikely legacy of a Liverpool slum childhood; he had kept his spirit, that of the tireless radical battler who never realizes which battles have been won, which abandoned, and which overtaken by the march of time; and he had kept his reputation. Everyone in the trade union movement knew McTeague; he was a legend – the legend of the poor boy who fights his way up, against all the odds; the legend of the political *guerilla* who uses any weapon that comes to his hand; the legend of the man who sparks trouble, and thrives on it, and makes something out of it.

There were many things to explain McTeague, and perhaps to excuse him. His family had been bitterly poor; he had watched his father, in those hungry thirties which had stained and dishonoured England, rusting away to nothing through lack of employment, lack of official interest, lack of anything savouring of hope. This degrading process had stolen the last twelve years of what should have been his father's full manhood. In reaction, McTeague had gone into union work, and found that it did some good. He had flirted with the Communists (there was some evidence that he had joined them), and found that this did some good also. Above all, he had fought, and fought again, to destroy what he hated; the image of his father, a silent bitter man shrunk into one corner of a cheerless kitchen, thrown onto a vast human scrap heap at the age of forty-five, and never leaving it until his body was brought down in decay.

McTeague had his reasons for fighting; in terms of the human reaction to indignity – rage and pity and resolution – they were valid. The trouble with McTeague was that trade union achievement had outstripped him; and this, instead of contenting him, had made him desperate. His tactics were as out of date as the poisoned arrow; his vocabulary, which he passed on to people like Vic Swann, was politically archaic. The great stalwarts of Labour – Keir Hardie, Ramsay MacDonald, Snowden – would have felt thoroughly at home with it. But that was four and five decades ago. Things had changed, out of all knowledge, for the better; and McTeague would never admit the fact – perhaps from atavistic fear, once again, of unemployment.

It was beyond question that he was the product of prolonged human debasement, and was entitled to show the wounds he bore. But from this debasement he had learned only one thing – how to pass the wounds on to other people.

It was possible to exaggerate his capacity for troublemaking, but not easy. Within the Seamen's Union, he had always been a thorn in the flesh of all who were ready for compromise; now that he was outside it, in the official sense, he still carried the fight wherever he could find the ground, with unremitting contempt for anyone who hinted that enough was enough. He had been a notable name on the Merseyside, when times were hard and the working man needed every friend he could find; he was still a notable name, but of a different sort.

When you said McTeague, you thought of the most dreary kind of indiscipline; 'token strikes' which could eat up a whole productive day, casual walkouts which delayed a sailing indefinitely, niggling disputes which, spreading to other unions and ending in a careless 'down tools', could double the cost of getting a ship to sea on time.

This was the kind of thing which McTeague could spark; which he *did* spark, on every possible occasion. People called him a lot of things; agitator, Communist, troublemaker, firebrand, champion of the working class, freedom fighter, friend of the little man, staunch ally of the underdog. It would be fairer, now, to call him an unqualified nuisance.

His nuisance value remained constant. Just as the squeaky wheel got the grease, so the man who screamed of injustice always found a lot of supporters. If the supporters in their turn found no evidence worth acting on, well, it was all on the right side, it was an act of eternal vigilance. Progressives could still rally round, confident that the watchdog of liberty had nabbed yet another burglar before he got to the swag.

McTeague had no principles save one, which could be summed up as 'To hell with the bosses'. Thus, when he now promised Norris that he would get him a ship, he meant, quite simply, that someone was going to pay for the crying scandal involved in denying Norris his simple democratic rights. Arguing whether Norris was a competent steward or a thieving shyster was beside the point; a typical boss-class red herring. The principle was clear; it was (as McTeague was fond of saying) as old as Magna Carta.

Norris was a worker; he was therefore entitled to full employment at a rising rate of pay; and he, McTeague, was going to get it for him.

Norris had brightened at McTeague's words; people usually brightened when McTeague spoke, unless they were on the other side of the table, in which case they either quailed before the onslaught or lost their tempers. But then Norris' natural pessimism, exemplified by his mournful face and (in a secondary way) his prematurely bald head, took over. He asked, suspiciously: 'When do I get this other ship? That's what I want to know.'

'Soon as I can work round to it,' said McTeague reassuringly. 'Like Comrade Wilby says, you're not a good case, not by yourself.' He saw that Norris, injured, was ready to argue the point, and he raised his hand. 'Don't think I'm counting you out. Justice is justice. You'll get your rights. The lads are all behind you. But I mean, you're not a good case where this particular ship is concerned. You're more of a' – he searched for a bolstering phrase, and found one without difficulty – 'more of a long-term project. It's the *Good Hope* I'm thinking of now. She's the one we want to stop.'

'Well, we did our best for you, yesterday,' put in Wilby, with a slight edge to his voice. 'Can't do more than down tools and walk off the job, can we? We was hoping for a sympathy strike. And we called a mass meeting. But what happened? Nothing.'

'Now, now,' said McTeague. 'Let's not split the ranks. You did a great day's work, no doubt about that, and it's appreciated. I give you my word, if I could have got the stewards out, I would have done it. But it wasn't the moment.'

'Any moment's the moment, far as I'm concerned,' said Wilby. But he was mollified by the compliment, and his voice lost its dissatisfied note. 'Don't forget we're always ready to do our bit for the movement, that's all.' He smiled foxily. 'I hear some of the stevedores were out doing their bit, last night.'

McTeague smiled, in the same confederate way. 'They say there was an accident, like.'

'Worst thing you ever saw.'

Barber, aware of an undercurrent, had perked up. 'What's all this about?'

'Haven't you heard?' said Wilby, in mock surprise. 'There was a nasty upset in the balance of payments ... It was down at Gladstone Dock,' he went on, with the relish of a man with a good story to tell. 'There was this car, see, all crated up and ready to load. Done up real posh. Consigned to His Royal Highness the Maharajah of something-or-other – you know, they call him the richest man in the world. Always doing the girls in nightclubs, the big layabout! Some of the lads was curious about it.

Wanted to know what it looked like. When a car's crated like that, there's bound to be something special inside.'

'Did they open the crate?' asked Barber.

'The very idea!' answered Wilby. 'You can't go round opening crates. The dock police would never forgive you ... But one of the loaders had a bit of bad luck with his fork-lifter. Trod on the accelerator instead of the brake. Tore the corner off the crate. You never saw such a mess. So the lads set out to clean it up.'

They waited, allowing Wilby his enjoyment.

'They cleaned it up, all right. Well, I mean, they had to pull off the broken bits, didn't they? So they were able to take a good look inside. And it's a special car, see, like they thought. Only it's a great big bloody Rolls-Royce, made of gold. That's all it was ... Well, not made of gold, exactly, but gold fittings stuck all over. Gold handles to the doors, gold knobs to everything, a running board with a gold edging for the slaves to stand on. And a lot more gold handles for them to hang on to while they were doing it. Must have cost a bleeding fortune – well, I know what it cost, because I saw the bill of lading. Eighteen thousand pounds, that's what it cost.'

'It's a crime,' said Norris, shocked. 'A bleeding crime, that's what it is. Eighteen thousand bloody pounds. And people out of work. People starving all over.'

'That's what the lads thought,' said Wilby. 'But they thought of it the other way round, see? They thought, this chap's got so much gold to chuck about, he won't miss a bit here and there. So they climbed in for a few souvenirs.' He laughed; he might have been there himself, joining in the fun. 'By the time they'd finished, it was just a plain ordinary car, fit for the likes of you and me. But if you see one of the lads with a couple of gold knobs on his telly, you'll know where he got them from.'

'What happened to the car?' asked Barber, after the laughter died down.

'Sent back to the works,' said Wilby. 'Minor repairs and adjustments … But it gives employment, doesn't it? That's what I like about it.'

'Good for the export trade, too,' said McTeague.

'Oh, aye. Two exports for the price of one.'

'Will they do anything about it?' asked Barber.

'Not they!' answered McTeague, contemptuously. 'Too scared. Good relations between management and labour – that's the motto now.'

'I wish it had been old Calderstone's car,' said Barber, brooding on it. 'I'd like to see him lose a bit of his gold plate.'

'What did he do to you, then?' asked Wilby.

'Oh, nothing much. He's just a snotty old bastard, that's all. Tried to argue the toss with me. All I wanted was a few straight answers.'

'I'll take care of Calderstone,' said McTeague grimly. 'He's top of my list.'

There was a noise below them, the banging of a door, the scraping of feet. They all listened as steps mounted the stairs. When they were halfway up, McTeague glanced at his watch.

'Might be Vic Swann,' he said. He turned towards the corner where the girl was. 'See who it is, love.'

Though the word 'love', in Lancashire, meant nothing more than day to day friendly greeting, it started a train of thought in Barber's mind, and he watched the girl as she obeyed McTeague, dog-like, and got up and moved across the room.

She was lumpish and slatternly, but pretty in a pasty sort of way; or she *had* been pretty, perhaps for one brief astonishing bout of love. Rumour said that it had been McTeague himself … Barber wondered if that were true, and if so, how long ago they had been lovers, and why it had happened in the first place, and whether it was a one-shot affair – accidental, regretted long before breakfast time – and how McTeague had managed to shift it from the bed to the desk, without upsetting either item of furniture; and what he thought about being stuck with her, and she with him. Or were they still comrades in arms, shoulder to shoulder in the great struggle ... But it wasn't a story really. Just background human interest.

The girl – whether lover, helpmeet, or millstone – had swung the door shut after her; and there was now a murmuring sound behind it, which those inside could not distinguish. Then she reappeared, and plodded forward, and made her dispirited report: 'It's a man from the papers.'

'Which paper?' asked Barber promptly.

'The Liverpool.'

McTeague had risen, with some alacrity; he shared with Lord Calderstone a taste for getting what space he could in the press. 'Anyone we know?' he asked.

'No.'

'I'd better see him, anyway. It can't do any harm.'

'Now just a minute,' said Barber. His fat face seemed ready to shrink down into peevishness. 'We've got an arrangement. Remember?'

'Of course I remember,' answered McTeague. 'I'm not going back on it. I won't give this chap anything. You know that.'

'Then why see him?'

McTeague spread his hands. 'Local paper. You know how it is. They're always on the doorstep. I don't want to get their backs up. I might need their help, one of these days.'

'Well, all right,' said Barber ungraciously. 'But just go slow, will you? I've got a story on this, and it's going to be *my* story. "Exclusive" means just what it says. And it's worth your while, anyway. Don't forget the coverage we can give you.'

'Take it easy,' said McTeague. 'You can listen, for all I care.' And to the girl, waiting in the centre of the room, part of the shabby furniture of his life: 'Show him in,' he said. 'Always glad to meet the press.'

The last words were spoken in a crisp, hearty, public relations voice; loud enough to carry through the closed doors. They should have provided a brisk entrance for the man waiting outside. He was, at least, no stranger to Barber; he was the Liverpool reporter who had shared the recent shipboard session with Lord Calderstone.

But he did not quite live up to the bouncing goodwill of the introduction. Once inside, he said: 'I'm Arkwright, from the *Liverpool Mail*,' and nodded his way round the room in an awkward series of salutes. Then he stood stock-still in the middle of the assembly. He was not exactly ill at ease, but he seemed to have no idea of what might be done or said next; it could never be a profitable basis for any interview. To Barber, whom he greeted last, he said: 'Hallo again,' in the manner of a man who invariably arrived late upon the scene. Everything he did or said proclaimed the young local reporter; fatally young, indisputably local, following a stray lead to a story which the big-time London villain had got to first.

Barber grunted in reply, ungraciously refusing the contact. If there was some freezing out to be done, he was going to do his share.

'Now let's see,' said McTeague cheerfully. 'I know a lot of you newspaper lads, but I haven't had the pleasure yet ... Can't offer you a chair, I'm afraid. We've got a full house today. What can I do for you?'

'I'd like to have a talk,' said Arkwright hesitantly. He looked round the assembled company, but he was a man without a magic wand; they still remained in evidence. 'Just a few questions. Is that OK?'

'Well, now,' said McTeague, with the same heartiness, 'I'm busy with a meeting, just at the moment. Is it anything special?'

'Oh no,' said Arkwright, ready to apologize. 'It's just – it's about the *Good Hope*.' He glanced at Barber, and away again. 'I was on board, a bit earlier, talking to Lord Calderstone. There was something about a strike mentioned. I wondered if you knew anything.'

'That was yesterday,' answered McTeague readily. 'But it wasn't a strike. What they call a jurisdictional dispute. Mr Wilby here' – he jerked his head – 'had to call a walkout on a very important question of principle. But it was fixed up this morning.'

'Scab labour,' said Wilby, with sour relish. 'We soon settled *that*.'

'No, I don't mean the ETU,' said Arkwright, who knew perhaps a little bit more than he was being given credit for. 'This is something else.' He plunged. 'Is it true that the stewards might be going to stage their own walkout?'

McTeague shook his head. 'I haven't heard anything about that. I can't help you there.'

'Oh.' Arkwright swallowed; his key question had not struck home; it had not struck anything. 'But there is some sort of unrest, isn't there?'

'There's unrest all over Merseyside,' said McTeague. 'There always will be, until the shipping companies give the lads a fair shake.'

'I mean, on board the *Good Hope*,' persisted Arkwright. 'They say she may not sail today.'

'I don't know anything about that,' answered McTeague. 'If I do hear, I'll let you know.'

Arkwright glanced at Barber again, trying, against all the odds, to add the thing up. 'Are you expecting any new developments?'

'Not so far as I know.'

'Can I wait till sailing time, then?'

McTeague shook his head again, with real regret. 'Like I said, we're in the middle of a meeting. It's not convenient, not just now. Tell you what – why don't you give me a ring, if you hear anything? Then maybe I'll be able to make a statement.'

'Well, all right ...' Arkwright swallowed once more, and found he did not like these meagre rations. 'But you know, I'd rather wait here, if that's OK. I can sit in the shop downstairs.'

In the silence that followed, Barber spoke. 'There's no point in waiting,' he said flatly, 'because there's no story. Nothing's going to happen here ... I think Mr McTeague wants to get back to work.'

At that, Arkwright suddenly came to life. He was young, and inexperienced; but he was making his way in the world, and he had already learned something in the hard school of newspaper tactics.

'I wasn't talking to you,' he said, in a sharp, nasal, Lancashire twang. His face grew pink as he summoned his courage for a rebuke. 'Just mind your own business ... This is a Liverpool story. There's Liverpool men involved ...' He turned back to McTeague. 'Is it true you're trying to stop the *Good Hope* sailing?'

'Now, now, lad,' said McTeague, peaceably. 'Don't take on. Mr Barber was only trying to make things easy for you. He didn't mean anything ... I tell you, I don't know anything about a steward's walkout. Or about stopping the sailing. That's a daft idea ... If I did know I'd be the first to tell you. You know me. I don't hide things from the press.

Never have and never will. You lads are too sharp, anyway ... If there's any developments, I'll let you know. All right?'

But Arkwright, once he had come to the boiling point of rebellion, was not one to simmer down so soon. He said, stubbornly: 'You can let me know now, if it's all the same to you,' and looked round the room. 'I'm not a fool,' he declared, perhaps for the first time in his life. 'There's a meeting going on here – you said so yourself. All right – what's the meeting about? You've got Mr Wilby – he led the ETU walkout yesterday. You've got Mr Norris – he's a steward, isn't he? He's the one that was sacked off the *Good Hope*.' He looked at the girl, and following the world's epitaph, found nothing to say. His glance came round to Barber, and he grew, if anything, pinker. 'Then you've got one of the national dailies, waiting around for something to happen.' He drew a deep breath. 'What's it all about? That's what I want to know.'

'I'll tell you what it's all about,' said Barber unpleasantly. His private ground, bought and paid for, was being threatened, and he reacted fiercely. 'It's a meeting, see? It was arranged a long time ago. We're discussing union matters. And it's by invitation only. And that's all there is to it.'

'It's not all, not by a long chalk!' said Arkwright bitterly. 'I know what you're up to! You've no right to try to make a closed shop out of this.'

'You've got a lot to learn,' said Barber. 'And that's the best I can say for you.'

At that, Arkwright, deflated, suddenly gave up. He turned away from Barber, and spoke to McTeague, on a subdued note with all the spirit run out of it. 'All right, if that's the way you want it ... But it's a Liverpool story all the same, like I said. And we've often backed the men before ... Don't blame me if it doesn't get proper treatment.'

'You've got the wrong end of the stick, lad,' said McTeague. 'But thanks all the same. And no hard feelings, eh!'

'We won't blame you,' said Barber. 'That's a promise.'

But Arkwright was already clear of the room, and on his way down the stairs, before Barber finished speaking. The brief storm had blown out.

McTeague expelled a long breath. 'Well ... You chaps certainly love each other, don't you?' But he was not really surprised, nor unadmiring; he knew all about people, supposedly in the same line of business, loving and not loving each other. Dog ate dog; men did not lag behind. 'All the same, I hope he won't go back in a temper and write a lot of tripe.'

'He won't write anything,' said Barber contemptuously. 'I know his sort. All wind and no doings. You can forget about Arkwright.'

Norris, a slow but determined thinker, finally spoke. 'But how did he know about me?' he asked querulously. 'Who's been talking about me?'

'Everybody knows about you,' answered McTeague, on a soothing note. 'I told you, you're a long-term project. And you'll be famous for it, one of these days.'

'In the meantime,' said Wilby, in the cold tones of a man left out of the current drama, 'we're not getting anywhere. What time was Vic Swann coming?'

'I don't know that he is coming, for certain,' said McTeague irritably. 'For Christ's sake, give us a chance to get our breath ... Vic Swann *was* coming, if he could get off. If not, he'll send a message.'

Barber, his head cocked to one side, said suddenly; 'That'll be him, now.'

He had been the first to hear the closing of the door below; now they all listened to the steps coming up the stairs. They were light bouncy steps, the steps of a man in a hurry, and confident that the hurry would be worthwhile. Not many such steps came up McTeague's stairs; mostly his visitors plodded or laboured or dragged their way upwards, loaded down by grievance. When McTeague said: 'That's Vic, all right,' he was only announcing a certainty.

Vic Swann came into the office like a breezy sparrow joining the gang in the stable yard; his raincoat flapping, his curly hair cresting on his forehead, his face as perky as a pound of buttons. He glanced quickly round, saw that he knew everyone in the room, and said facetiously: 'Hallo, soaks – I mean folks! Keeping nice, isn't it? Who was the chap in all the hurry?'

'What chap?' asked McTeague.

Vic Swann shrugged. 'I dunno. That's why I'm asking. Shot out of the front door, a moment ago. Went past me like a dose of salts.'

'Oh, him ... Chap from the newspapers.'

'What did you give him, then? Must have been a red hot story.'

'I gave him nothing,' said McTeague, 'and he didn't like it at all ... Take your coat off, lad. How's it going on board?'

'Same load of tripe.' Vic Swann tossed his coat onto a peg, sat down on one edge of the oilcloth table top, and pulled out a crumpled packet of cigarettes. Through a cloud of smoke he said: 'Treating us like a bit of dirt, as usual. I'm fed up with it.'

'Anything special?' asked Barber.

'Well, you know ...' Vic Swann hesitated, then shrugged again; the gesture of a man too big to bother with details. Finally he said: 'It's the system, see? If you're not one of the bosses, they push you about like a bunch of kids. Talk about wage slaves ... There's no future in that job, and the lads all know it. There never will be a future, till we get a fair deal.'

'That's what I say,' Norris chimed in. 'Just look at my case. Rank injustice! Given the sack for taking a bite of cheese.'

McTeague nodded, more towards Barber than anyone else. 'I told you, the men are in an ugly mood. They've been pushed too far. They've about reached the limit. Question is, how we can help them.'

Wilby said: 'You've got to have a dispute.'

'What do you mean, dispute?' countered Vic Swann aggrievedly. 'It's all disputes all the time. And it's answering the bell all the time. And it's running errands all the time. How would you like to be at the beck and call of a lot of old layabouts, twenty-four hours of the day?' He assumed a mincing tone, raised an imaginary lorgnette. 'Oh, steward! Bring me my smelling salts. I feel a little faint. And put my rug straight – my feet are freezing! And do, do try to remember about my bath water. Never more than eighty-four degrees – I'm tired of telling you! And please ask the Captain what's for dinner tonight. And tell the orchestra not to play so loud. It's going right through my head!'

But Wilby was not going to share the limelight with this talented performer. 'I mean, a proper case,' he broke in curtly. 'Like unfair treatment, or victimization, or overtime. Like what we had with your uncle, yesterday. That was a real dispute.' He smirked briefly; it had been his own, his very own. 'Something you can do something about.'

As Swann said nothing, McTeague asked him: 'Have you talked to your uncle? Or has he talked to you?'

'He's always talking to me,' answered Vic Swann. 'Like they call a Dutch uncle, i'nt it? He's another one I'm fed up with.'

'How's that?'

'Oh, he's always going on about everything. Take it easy – give it a try – things aren't so bad – you should have seen it in the old days. Trouble is, he's got a lot of the lads thinking the same way.'

'As long as he hasn't got you thinking that way.'

'You know me,' said Vic Swann. 'Solidarity forever.'

'Good lad, Vic ... You won't get anywhere, listening to Tom Renshaw. I've got to put it like that, even if he is your own uncle. There's new ideas coming along. Chaps like him went out with the ark.'

'Don't look at me,' answered Vic Swann defensively. 'It isn't me that listens to him.'

But McTeague had some points to make, and he could not resist an audience. 'It's your dad you want to think of,' he said. 'Hardly remember him, do you? Killed in the war, wasn't he? Well, I remember him ... Of course he was killed in the war. Merchant seaman – lots of them got killed.' He pointed a dramatic finger. 'And lots of them didn't! Just that your dad wasn't one of the lucky ones, that's all. He was marked out to be killed, years before. For one reason, and one reason only. You know what it was? Because he was out of work before the war, for *five years*. Just doing nothing, living on bread and marge and tea, wasting away. Then suddenly they give him a job. Funny thing – they can always find jobs in wartime. But what use was he, at the end of five years on the dole? What was he like? I'll tell you, because I saw him. He was skin and bone, that's what he was. But he was good enough to get killed in the war. So they give him this job, after five years turning their backs on him. Deck hand on a tanker. Ought to be grateful, didn't he? But the tanker's torpedoed. And your dad's drowned, when everyone else is picked up. You know why he was drowned? Because you can't swim when you've been starved to death for five years.' The pointing finger came darting out again. 'I tell you, the capitalist system killed your dad! And that's why we've got to kill the capitalist system!'

The practised oratory reached its natural pause; the recital, moving, undoubtedly valid in spite of its brush-strokes of exaggeration, came roundly to the end of a chapter. McTeague faced his audience, as he had done thousands of times before – from platforms, from the backs of lorries, from workbenches, from a dozen vantage points. He seemed to be expecting something from them, even if it were only a murmur of 'He's right!'; and Vic Swann, the awkward focus of all this, gave it to him.

'I know he was out of work, and all,' he said lamely. 'My Ma used to tell me.'

'What did she say about it?' The finger pointed again, jabbing for emphasis. 'More important still, what does she say about it now?'

Vic Swann paused before mumbling: 'She says things aren't like that any more.'

McTeague jumped on it, and from it; he still had some way to go, and he was glad of the springboard. 'I don't want to contradict your Ma, lad, but we know better than that, don't we? Things *are* like that! What about a fair chance for everybody? What about inequality? D'you think we've got rid of that?' Half his attention was towards Barber, who was scribbling a note. 'Just you tell me something. How many do you sleep in a cabin?'

'Eight.'

'And how many sleep in Lord Bloody Calderstone's luxury suite?'

'Just him.'

'There you are, you see. Discrimination! One old man in one cabin, and eight of the lads living like pigs in another. There's still a privileged class, and don't you forget it. We've got to get rid of it, once and for all!' His voice softened momentarily; the *vox humana* stop was pulled out, for a brief couple of sentences. 'Like I told you, I knew your dad. I knew how he lived and how he died. And I felt for you, Vic, because my dad was out of work, too. Only he died out of work – they didn't even fatten him up for the war.' The voice gained strength again; it was the peroration, the bit that got the cheers and the vote of confidence and the mass call for strike action. 'Of course things are better now – there'd have been a revolution else – but the system's still the same! All they did was give way a bit, because they had to. But it can still happen again. It can happen to you! Don't think you're safe, because you get a few bob a week extra, and an eight-hour day instead of sixteen. They'll take it away from you, any time they feel strong enough, any time they can find the excuse. That's why we've got to fight! That's why we've got to be masters! Then we can call the tune ourselves, and it'll be the sweetest tune you ever heard!'

He had done very well, and he knew it from their expressions. Norris, hanging on every word, had dropped his mouth open; the cynical Wilby had been nodding his approval of each point. Even Barber seemed to have found it worthwhile to listen, and to make a note or two on his scribbling pad. Only the girl, slouched over her typewriter, had heard nothing that struck any chord.

For her, it was another dull skein of life, another flow of words. 'He's playing our tune,' she might have thought, in secret rapture, months or years earlier. But now she did not hear the tune; no melody, not even a sad one, lingered on. She had heard only her own eternal song; the sound of her typewriter, and the dock traffic on the cobblestones below, and men talking. There was nothing new in any of that; nothing to raise a girl's head, nor her hopes, nor her heart.

But the song had struck Vic Swann in quite another way. Suddenly he was all cockiness again, and ready for any battle in this great cause. 'Now you're talking!' he said determinedly. 'That's more like it ... You just say what you want me to do, and I'll do it.'

He was speaking, of course, to McTeague; but McTeague was not ready with an answer. Speech could promote action, but it could not take its place; a discourse on what to think was not the same as a crisp directive on what to do. He said: 'Let me think about it a bit, Vic,' and dropped his head in his hands, leaving his audience with a view of nothing more than a blank grey bush of hair. With the prophet thus withdrawn, Barber looked up from his scribbling pad, and spoke to Vic Swann: 'You said you were sleeping eight to a cabin. How big is the cabin?'

Vic Swann, brought down to a mundane level, was not ready with an answer, either. 'I dunno,' he said, offhand. Then he grew conscious of his audience, and of Barber's poised pencil. 'Just one of the crew cabins, I suppose you'd call it. But it's crowded enough, and that's a fact. Bunks all around, and a little bit of a table in the middle. Proper pigsty, it is, in bad weather.' He grinned self-consciously. 'Better not mention my name, though. You'll be getting me the sack.'

Barber nodded abstractedly; he was not probing for fact, so much as seeking extra edge for a tale already told, a knife already honed. He now had his notes for the first half of his story. By way of contrast with the Calderstone interview, he had jotted down 'Continual unrest among the crew' and 'Burning resentment against superiors' and 'Men in ugly mood' and 'Seething discontent against harsh living conditions'; and he now felt free to add: 'A young steward, who asked that his name be withheld, for fear of reprisals, said that the *Good Hope* was "an absolute pigsty", with eight men crowded into a single tiny cabin, and the food "not fit for dogs". He contrasted this with palatial suites, occupied by one luxury-class passenger, costing £500 for a single voyage. "It's out-and-out slavery," he told me bitterly.

"I've had enough of it!" So much for the background to today's strike action, which has tied up the ill-named *Good Hope* for yet another twenty-four hours.'

He added 'Passenger reaction', and closed his pad with a snap. The libel department would have to take care of some of it. But only McTeague and Swann themselves could take care of the second half of the story – if there was to be a second half, if his exclusive was going to come true.

As if in answer to his prompting, McTeague raised his head, ready once more for decision and command.

'Comrade Wilby's right,' he said. 'We've got to have a dispute. It doesn't need to be a big one. Anything will do. Just as long as it starts the ball rolling again.'

'We haven't got much, right now,' said Wilby sourly. 'Not what I'd call a dispute.'

'Well, we'll just have to make one, then.'

'What about my case?' asked Norris. 'There's barefaced injustice for you.'

'It's not quite what we want,' answered McTeague. 'And it's not new, either.' He looked across at Vic Swann. 'I reckon we've got to leave it to Vic.'

'Suits me,' said Vic Swann. 'Just tell me how to go about it.'

'I'll tell you,' said McTeague readily. 'But just do it right, that's all. First thing, you go back on board, and pick some sort of a quarrel ... What's the name of that Chief Steward the lads are all complaining about?'

'Bryce,' said Vic Swann. 'Mr Bloody Bryce, the bosses' stooge.'

'That's the one,' said McTeague. 'Get into a row with Bryce – a big row, the sort he has to do something about. Doesn't matter what it is. But make it something he has to bring up before the Staff Commander. Or the Captain, even. You'll be disciplined, but don't you fret about that. We'll get you out of it, all right. Then go down to the messdeck, and get the lads together, and hold a meeting. Tell them what's happened, and call for a walkout.' He looked at his watch. 'It's four o'clock. You haven't much time – only about two hours – but that works in our favour. It'll be a rush job. Even if you can get half the stewards off the ship for an hour or so, they'll have to postpone the sailing again. Then we'll see what we can do, from this end. We'll back you up, anyway.'

'Same here,' said Wilby, with more relish. 'Call a sympathy strike, that's what we'll do. We'll show 'em what solidarity is!'

Vic Swann was frowning. 'Well, all right,' he said uncertainly. 'But what sort of a row?'

'Leave that to you,' answered McTeague. 'Make a complaint about the food – or the overcrowding – or Bryce's bullying – there's a dozen ways. God knows there's enough to complain about, on that ship! Like I said, make a row, get yourself into trouble.' He raised a warning finger. 'Only one thing, though – don't start a fight, or use force, or anything like that. If you do, you'll spoil it all. We've got to keep this legal.'

'That Bryce,' said Vic Swann. 'I'd like to knock his block off.'

'Well, don't knock his block off,' said McTeague. 'I told you, keep it legal. Any fool can go to jail, and then where will we be? The ship will be halfway downriver, while they're still marching you up the landing stage to be charged.' He tapped his finger on the table in front of him, six separate times, as he emphasized each point. 'Get this straight, now. Have a row. Get yourself hauled up before the Staff Commander. Listen to the punishment. Go back and tell the lads about it. Then lead them off the ship ... She can't sail with half the catering staff ashore, and the rest refusing to start the trip short-handed.'

Barber, the knowing man of the world, was now a little less than happy at what he seemed to have a hand in. 'You've got to be careful about this,' he said to McTeague. 'It isn't the same thing as a genuine grievance. It's getting a bit more involved than I – '

'Of course it's a genuine grievance!' interrupted McTeague forcefully. 'Just you wait. Whatever it is, it'll be genuine all right, you mark my words. I tell you, this has been going on for a long time. We've had just about all the trouble we want from the *Good Hope*. I'm sick of her, and a lot of other things besides. She's a rotten ship, and Hope Lines is a rotten company, and we're going to get it all changed, or know the reason why. Vic is only bringing things to a head, that's all.'

'Well,' said Barber. 'OK, then.'

McTeague turned to Vic Swann. 'That's it, lad. You stop her from sailing, and we'll take it from there. But don't forget, we're counting on you. If you *can* stop her, it'll be the best day's work you ever did.'

Vic Swann lifted his coat from the peg by the door, and made ready to leave. 'Watch my smoke,' he said cockily. And then, in a falsetto parody of Gracie Fields' voice: '*Wish me luck, as you wave me goodbye,*' he trilled. Then, with a toss of his head, he was gone.

In the silence, Barber wrinkled his nose. 'Haven't heard that tune for a long time.'

McTeague answered what Barber had not said: 'Oh, he'll do all right. Just you wait ... Don't forget, the *Good Hope's* got a new captain, just come up from the cargo ships. This'll be the first time he's been in proper trouble. He'll have to be a genius to handle it.'

'Perhaps he *is* a genius,' said Barber.

'He's a sailor,' said McTeague. 'Wood from the neck up, and scared to death of losing his pension. I know his sort. He's not going to sail short-handed, he's not going to risk a flaming row on his first passenger command, and he's not going to know how to deal with this, either.' He sat back, and stretched. 'Leave it to Vic Swann,' he said. 'He'll get us some action.'

'Then it'll be our turn again tomorrow,' said Wilby. He smoothed back his yellow quiff of hair. 'We're going to tie this ship up in knots, between us.'

Peace – an interim, waiting peace – had settled on the room. Barber, relaxing also, lit a cigarette. Then he strolled to the window, and looked down onto the dreary Liverpool street outside. It ran east and west, turning its back on the docks, but it could not exclude them. This was still the heart of a great port; here, men and ships were closely involved; here the pressure of the land met the pressure of the sea. Out of that classic contest, history was made, stories were written, reporters won fame ... He turned away again, satisfied, hopeful.

'Looks like there's a very good chance,' he said, and settled down to wait.

CHAPTER THREE

The Man in the Middle

❖

Hope Lines took good care of their captains. Considering that the maintenance, operation, and control of a 25,000-ton ship costing eight million pounds called for a good man, they went to some trouble to find that good man and, when found, to cherish him according to his worth. The Captain's quarters on board the *Good Hope* reflected this conviction that the man who took most of the strain and all of the responsibility should not have to worry about mere creature comforts.

The company allowed him two hundred and fifty square feet of well-appointed living space – which, for a sailor, was luxury indeed. They gave him a sleeping cabin with a separate bathroom; a day cabin with a bar, a hi-fi radio set, and wall-to-wall Axminster carpeting; and a pantry to keep his food hot and his drinks cold. They gave him his own steward – one of the prize jobs on board. On the business side of the ledger, they provided him with a direct telephone to the bridge, an intercom linking him with the Staff Commander, the Purser, and the Chief Engineer, a barometer, a wind velocity indicator, a repeater compass to check the course, a miniature radar scan to check the navigation, and a somewhat superfluous gadget which showed how far the ship was rolling in either direction.

Having thus done their very best for him – as a sailor and as a man – they expected to receive, in return, the highest standard of seamanship, discipline, and general competence. We look after you, Hope Lines seemed to be saying; now you look after our ship, and our passengers, and our maritime reputation.

Captain Blacklock, master of the *Good Hope*, was very conscious of this implicit bargain, as he sat at his desk in the day cabin, and went methodically through the endless series of papers which were part of every sailing. It was the best cabin he had ever occupied, and the *Good Hope* the finest ship he had yet commanded; but he felt – indeed, he knew – that his appointment was something of a fluke, a stroke of sailor's luck, and he had not yet got over the surprise, nor fully taken it in.

He knew exactly what was expected of him, and much of it posed no problem save that of stamina. The *Good Hope* represented 25,000 tons of work and worry; she had to leave on time, dock punctually at the end of eight days, run smoothly, sail without incident, keep away from trouble and the wrong kind of publicity, and make a profit for the owners. This was any captain's job; Blacklock knew he could do it, because he had been trained for it since he was a sixteen-year-old apprentice. But with a ship like this one, he had to be a lot of other things besides a competent seaman; he had to be, at the very least, a businessman, a diplomat, a social success, and an industrial negotiator.

At this particular moment, he did not like the prospect; secretly he was not sure if he were ready for it, in spite of all the preparation; he doubted if he could do it really well. Command of the *Good Hope* was, at this stage, the crown of his professional life; and the crown, on its first fitting, seemed weighty, and over-ornate, and top heavy in its daunting majesty.

He signed his name at the foot of a manifest, and shrugged, and turned to the next batch of papers. Whatever his private thoughts and fears, the job was here, and must be faced. Whatever he felt about it, it was not going to show.

Blacklock was forty-six; a tough, stocky man who had come up the hard way. He had served a long apprenticeship with Hope Lines, which saw to it that its future captains sampled all the available jobs before receiving the final accolade – command of one of their big passenger liners. In the last five years, Blacklock had been the Chief Officer of the *Majestic Hope,* and Staff Commander of the *Grand Hope*, both sister ships of the one in which he now sat; then he had graduated to command of his own ship, but (again in accordance with Hope Lines tradition) she was only a medium-sized freighter, plying the North Atlantic run and taking sixteen days on the trip instead of eight.

He would still have been in that job, without prospect of advancement for a long time, had it not been for three separate accidents.

Within the last month, one Hope Lines captain had died; a second had fractured his hip on a rolling dance floor (a typical hazard, the subject of a special insurance clause); and a third had gone to hospital a week earlier with all the symptoms of a fatal cancer. Thus the endemic promotion block, the log jam of professional advance, had suddenly broken; three new captains were needed, for the three big ships which kept Hope Lines on the North Atlantic map. Blacklock was third in line of seniority, and his credentials were impeccable; and so, five years earlier than he had any right to expect, he now sat in the Captain's cabin of the *Good Hope*, and made ready for his first voyage.

The programme of that first voyage, on paper, seemed simple; yet the more one looked at it, the more the problems multiplied. The *Good Hope* had lost twenty-four hours already; therefore they must sail today – in fact they must sail within the next two hours, so as to catch the tide over the Mersey Bar. Then they had to make a quick trip across the Atlantic; an absolute maximum of eight days, and seven if possible, must see them in New York. There they had to disembark their passengers, discharge 4,000 tons of assorted cargo, victual-up according to cruise standards, embark six hundred and fifty new holidaymakers, and sail on their first Caribbean cruise, all within thirty-six hours.

Many different things could go amiss. They might have a slow passage across the Atlantic, and lose another day, or even two; the met forecast was not exactly wonderful. They might have to dock without tugs in New York; there were rumours of a tug strike there. The discharge of cargo, and the taking on of fresh stores, might lag behind schedule. Above all, they might never leave Liverpool in the first place, if all the rumours – particularly about a stewards' walkout – turned out to be true. In that case, they would be late in sailing, later still at New York, and too late altogether for the start of the cruise, which would have to be cancelled.

Cruises made money; cancelled cruises made a murderous loss. If all the worst things happened, he, Captain Blacklock, would start his new, upgraded passenger career with one of the biggest black marks in the history of the line. It was unfair, but so was income tax, and the price of whisky, and the doctrine of original sin. The black mark would stay with him for the rest of his working life.

In actual fact, this was not his chief worry. He was familiar with such problems; he had met them before, though not as a captain; he had watched other captains wrestling with sailing delays, threatened strikes, bad weather, bad luck; and he had learned from his watching. Now he could do as he had been trained to do – absorb the setbacks, take the hard knocks, and buffet his way through. But there were other areas in which he was not confident, and probably never would be. One of them – perhaps the major one – was the social side of a ship such as the *Good Hope*.

To begin with, there was Lord Calderstone; Chairman of the line, big man in any league, and possibly the most formidable passenger any Hope Lines captain could have on board his ship. Lord Calderstone would be an ever-present factor at the Captain's table. He would have access to the bridge in any weather, and the *entrée*, at any time of his own choosing, to the Captain's private cabin.

He would always be there, the trained observer, not so much taking notes – no man of Lord Calderstone's calibre need descend to the vulgarity of taking notes – as passing a definite judgement on Blacklock's ability to command. If Blacklock did well, he was only measuring up to the Hope Lines standard. If he made a mess of it, he would be doing so under the cold eye of a hanging judge.

Then there was the matter of the Caribbean cruises, which would still lie ahead of him, even after he had passed his first test. There were to be three of these, lasting a month each; three times in quick succession his ship would be invaded by a fresh set of passengers intent on carefree pleasure, and he, the Captain, would be the focus of that entertainment. Mostly they would be Americans, and therefore avid for the refinements of service which they could never get in their own country; service was something which the Americans demanded, and the British gave, and both sides by now knew their respective places.

He, as Captain, would have to walk a smiling tightrope of public relations affability. If he were too approachable, he would cheapen his image, and talking to the Captain would be like talking to a bus driver – unremarkable, part of the trip, included in the price of the ticket. On the other hand, if he were too reserved, it would be set down as just another example of British stuffiness, and the word would quickly spread: 'Next time, go French Lines – they really know how to treat the customers.'

Somewhere in between, poor old Captain Blacklock could be left far behind; and Hope Lines would also be left far behind, and people like Lord Calderstone, noting the fact, would put a little red ink cross against his name, before calling for a list of men more likely to succeed.

Blacklock found himself shrugging his shoulders again, an unusual reaction. Perhaps it was to be a shrugging sort of day, a day of what-can't-be-cured-must-be-endured. The problems, great and small, had to be dealt with in sequence. And probably, he thought, one of them had to be dealt with now, as it moved into his cabin in the person of Staff Commander Martin.

In the twenty-odd years since they had started to move up the ladder together, he and Martin had never liked each other, and things were not now likely to improve. Perhaps the friction was inevitable; the two of them were near contemporaries in a highly competitive world, and Martin, a few months his junior, was next on the list for a Hope Lines command. He was a smoother man than Blacklock, a better-spoken, better-looking man; a good seaman (Blacklock would give him that much) and far more polished in the social sense (Blacklock would give him that much, too, and welcome). Martin was a wonderful party man, whereas Captain Blacklock was not a party man at all.

In fact, they were two different kinds of animal, and they had been watching each other for a long time, warily treading the same tract of forest which held the same traps for both, the same pitfalls and dangers, and the same rewards for the wide awake. Perhaps there were going to be deeper differences, now that they were in closer contact. In the last four days, since he took over command of the *Good Hope*, Blacklock had noted a certain attitude in Martin; it was not insolence – he was not the insolent type – but a consciousness of superiority, as if it were beyond doubt that only a matter of luck had made Blacklock the Captain, and Martin his Staff Commander.

There was a certain slowness in the way that Martin said 'sir', which seemed to imply that, but for those few months' difference in seniority, it would have been the other way round, and that the other way round would have been the natural way round, the preferable way round, because he, Martin was better fitted for command and should have been given the *Good Hope*.

There could be some truth in that, thought Blacklock, as he looked up and nodded to Martin. They were virtually equal in merit, and he himself had had the luck of the draw. But that, he thought more forcefully, just about summed it up. Good luck or bad, he *was* the Captain and Martin *was* the Staff Commander, and that was the way they were going to whistle this particular tune.

Martin, entering at a leisurely pace, had put some papers on the Captain's desk. Now he said: 'Watch-and-Quarter Bill, sir,' as if he could not recall whether Blacklock knew what a Watch-and-Quarter Bill was. There was also, once again, a definite slowness about the word 'sir', and Blacklock suddenly decided that the time had come to react. If this were to be a day for dealing with problems one at a time, it could be a pleasure to start with this one.

He nodded again, and said: 'Thanks,' in as brief a tone as possible. Then, as Martin seemed to be waiting, he asked: 'Something else?'

'No,' answered Martin easily. 'I just wondered if there was anything I could do.'

The Captain did not like the implication, and felt ready to show it. 'You've got your job, haven't you?'

'Oh yes,' said Martin, as if his job were something any capable man could do with one hand in his spare time. 'I only meant – well, you know, all the extra work of taking over. If there's anything'

'You do your job,' said Blacklock curtly. 'I'll do mine. That way we'll get along.'

It had sounded crude, as it was meant to, but Martin did not seem put out; he was preserving the poise of the man who always makes allowances for other, more harassed humans. 'Of course we'll get along,' he said pleasantly, and added: 'sir,' after so long an interval that notice had to be taken of it.

The Captain sat back, and looked squarely at him. 'Now let's get this straight. We both know what it's all about, so it better come out in the open. I've been promoted, you haven't. Your turn'll come, but it hasn't come yet. We're dealing with *now* – today, this minute, this ship. I'm the Captain, you're my Staff Commander. That's the way it's going to be, and the sooner you get used to it, the better I'll like it.'

When he got angry, which was rarely, Martin went pink; and he went pink now, as he took in the drift of Blacklock's curt phrases. After a moment he said: 'I honestly don't know what this is all about ... I hoped we could work things out so that – '

'There's nothing to work out,' interrupted Blacklock. 'When I want you to work something out, I'll let you know. In the meantime, just you take care of your department, and let's have a little less of the helping hand stuff. I don't like it, and I don't need it.'

'Honestly, I don't understand what – ' Martin began again.

'Shut up!' snapped Blacklock suddenly. 'I didn't say I wanted to make a discussion out of it. I'm just telling you what to do.'

'Yes, sir,' said Martin.

'Is there anything more to report about the stewards?'

'No, sir.' Now Martin's tone was sulky. 'There's nothing new there.'

'What's the position, then?'

'Bryce says they're still talking, but that's about all. One of them's ashore, seeing McTeague, so they say. I don't know if it means anything. The rest of them just seem to be waiting to see what happens.'

'Who's the one ashore?'

'Swann. Tourist steward.'

'Log him when he comes back. He's got no business ashore, just before sailing.'

'Well, sir …' Martin was back to his easy manner again, the role of the diplomatic adviser. 'I was going to overlook it, this time. I don't think we want to risk starting anything, at this stage.'

'Log him,' repeated the Captain. 'I'll decide whether we're going to start anything.'

'Very well, sir,' said Martin, infuriatingly reasonable. 'I just thought that was what you meant by taking care of my department.'

The Captain let it go by, for the moment; the mutual abrasion, the ebb and flow of moods and attitudes, could become interminable. Instead he said: 'If this chap's talking to McTeague, that could mean trouble. *He's* the one we've got to watch out for. He's only waiting for a chance to call a walkout.'

'I suppose that could happen,' said Martin.

'You don't sound too sad about it.'

'Sir?'

'The prospect of the stewards walking out doesn't seem to worry you.'

Martin's expression was wonderfully injured. 'Sir, I thought you were taking over responsibility for that.'

Blacklock glared back at him. 'Are you trying to be funny?'

'No, sir. I'm not trying to be – funny.'

That settled it, thought the Captain, in sudden overwhelming anger. He had a slight Liverpool accent, especially in moments of stress, and he had pronounced the word nearer to 'foony' than 'funny'; and Martin, who invariably spoke the purer tones of the Southern Counties, had gone so far as to copy his pronunciation. It had hit his only sensitive nerve. Enough was enough, he decided; if the direct clash had to come, it might as well be a good one, and it might as well be now. Apparently, in spite of a tough line, he had not yet made himself clear.

He barked out: 'Martin!' and as the other man stiffened at the tone, he continued: 'That's enough from you! Stop fooling about, or you'll be in real trouble! The catering staff is *not* my responsibility. It's yours, and don't you forget it.'

'Very well, sir.'

'If there's unrest, I expect to hear about it. From you. If one of the stewards is breaking the rules, I want him logged.' He was staring fixedly at Martin. 'I'm new to the *Good Hope*, but I'm not new to anything else. I'm not taking any sauce from you. And I'm not running this ship on soft soap and guesswork, either. If there's a chance of a strike, we won't avoid it by looking the other way. Is that clear?'

'Yes, sir,' answered Martin, subdued. 'I'll do my best.'

'You'd better,' said the Captain grimly. 'Otherwise, that steward chap isn't the only one who's going to be logged.' And as Martin, shaken at last, looked at him with the beginnings of true alarm: 'That's all,' said the Captain, almost cheerfully. 'Let me know immediately if there's any new developments.'

It had been a pleasure, as he had expected, and he felt the better for it; but it had left a sour taste, nonetheless. Ships did not run smoothly, when the two top men were thus wrestling with each other; a Captain who could not rely absolutely on his Staff Commander must keep watching him all the time, and a lot of other men on board, also watching, would note the fact, and spread rumours, and take sides, and give a little less than their best because they had this thing on their minds instead of the thing they were meant to be doing.

The situation would affect Martin most of all, because he would never forget the incident, nor its outcome. From this moment forward, he would go to work on it, slowly and subtly, so that in the end the defeat might be wiped out, and the advantage regained. There were a dozen ways, from an inflexion of the voice to an order carried out with minimum zeal, in which Martin could promote his own cause. Martin would find them all, and use them all, because he was that kind of man, and the relationship between them had become that kind of relationship.

But there were other things which had emerged from the conversation; real things, as opposed to foolish occasions of friction. The Captain had said: 'You don't sound too sad about it,' when Martin had spoken of the prospect of a stewards' walkout, and of course the comment had been true; Martin, especially in his present mood, would be far from heartbroken to see a rival captain – that was how he would think of it – running into trouble and making a mess of his first voyage. He would never actively engage in sabotage, which was too dangerous, but he would not exactly break his neck in coming to the rescue, if a crisis developed. Judiciously neutral, he would sit back, contribute a not-too-private running commentary on the course of misfortune, and enjoy the sport.

He was not sad about it, nor was the Captain sad about it; instead, he was angry. He was angry for the sake of his ship, and for his discomfited passengers, and for the stupid untidiness of it all. There had been so much of this sort of thing in the last few years, and Hope Lines had had a sizeable share of it; at times it seemed as if they were simply living from voyage to voyage – *somehow* sailing on time, *somehow* keeping to a schedule, *somehow* avoiding the big crisis which could tie a ship up and – most disgraceful of all – result in her passengers having to fly to their destinations at the company's expense.

The Captain was past thinking of these manoeuvres as stupid; now they seemed to him to be malicious, destructive, almost criminal in their disregard for the facts of maritime life. By now, these people must know perfectly well that they could bring any shipping line to bankruptcy, and destroy their own jobs in the process; and yet they went on doing it with the same half-doped readiness, as if it were habit-forming, like beer and television and Saturday night sex.

They listened to the men who didn't give a damn whether a ship sailed or not, as long as they could exercise the power which industrial evolution had thrown their way. They listened and, like any other brand of silly sheep, they obeyed. Then they put their hands in their pockets and leant back, the easier to listen to another set of men telling them: 'The unemployment figures are a national disgrace!'

They were like children – but bloody-minded children, with a frightening adult strength, capable of wrecking their country instead of their toys. They were now part of his job, in a way they had never been before; the *Good Hope* had to sail in two hours, and the *Good Hope* was his ship, and no one else's, and if he did not acquit himself well, on this occasion and on all the other occasions which were going to crop up for the first year or two of his new status, then it could be goodbye to the passenger trade, and goodbye to the rank of Commodore of the Line, which was his most secret ambition, and back to the cargo haul and the low rungs of a ladder which would no longer lead anywhere except towards the modest decay of retirement.

He had the power and the will to rise; but the rest was luck – an awful lot of luck, at just the right moments. And as if to make this point in the most dramatic way possible, there was now a double knock on the door, and his steward, a man with a sense of occasion which sometimes outran the facts, announced in accents of absolutely regal consequence: 'Captain, sir – Lord Calderstone!'

Lord Calderstone entered the Captain's cabin in a way which Blacklock himself could never have managed. Of course he had an appreciable start, where the Captain was concerned; he was tall, distinguished, and rich, whereas the Captain was short, rather plain, and salaried on the Hope Lines scale. But there was much more to it than that; the phrase 'To the manner born' sprang instantly to mind; this was not just someone coming into a room – it was an entrance, made by a man whose every attitude, from the angle of his jaw to the firm tread of his feet, seemed to proclaim that the room was the better for his presence.

Aristocrats could do this, thought Captain Blacklock enviously, as he rose to greet his guest; it was something you were blessed with, like blue eyes or lots of hair, and you could not fake it, nor copy it, nor do without it. When Lord Calderstone greeted him, there was no doubt who was the *grand seigneur* and who was the humble tenant.

Nor was there any undue emphasis on it; that would have been superfluous. 'My dear fellow!' said Lord Calderstone, with all the ease in the world. 'I just looked in, and I've no intention of wasting more than a few moments of your time. But first of all, congratulations!'

It was insincere, of course – in the world of Lord Calderstone, promotion to command of a ship was roughly equivalent to advancement from Head Teller to Chief Cashier – but it was also irresistible. Captain Blacklock found himself immediately warmed by the friendly greeting; in a rosy glow of gratitude, he exclaimed 'Thank you, sir!' as breathlessly as any schoolboy who, having won the high jump, is treated to a kindly pat on the back from the games master. Then, the civilities done, he made bold to offer Lord Calderstone a drink.

'Well, now,' said Lord Calderstone, judiciously, as if he were weighing, at the very least, some fantastic takeover bid involving six million pounds, 'I must think seriously about that, mustn't I? Got to watch this shipboard hospitality, you know. I've had at least one more than my midday quota already. Don't want to start the voyage on the wrong foot. But yes – I think I *will* have a very small whisky and water.'

This also was a constructive pack of lies. Lord Calderstone's head for liquor was magnificent, tested and proved at a hundred banquets, parties, and late-night negotiating sessions; he was as likely to show himself publicly affected by alcohol as he was to be guilty of indecent exposure. His byplay was part of the promotion treatment, the Captain realized, as he summoned his steward, and the steward poured the drinks; it was the part designed to put the Captain at his ease, to show he was now included in Lord Calderstone's version of the human race.

There would no doubt be other aspects to this meeting, which was a mixture of courtesy, inquiry, and therapy. But it was probable that Lord Calderstone was there to observe, in preference to all the rest; he was now engaged in getting his first impression of Blacklock in the role of Captain, for though he had met him before, he had never yet observed him under the limelight of command. The Captain was not therefore surprised when Lord Calderstone bent an inquiring eye upon him, and asked: 'How are you settling in?'

There were all sorts of possible answers, ranging from the non-committal to the buoyant; Blacklock did not feel like giving any of them. He was not an operator, like Staff Commander Martin; he was a sailor, with a sailor's preference for a plain tale and a minimum of colouring matter. He had a job to fill, and a ship to run, and he could only do his best. Impressing Lord Calderstone was part of that job, but it was not the important part; it was the froth on the top, and if there were nothing under the froth, he was going to lose the job anyway. He answered, unsmiling: 'So far, everything's gone well. She's the biggest ship I've ever had, which means there's more to go wrong. But then, I've got more people to help me ... That's about the size of it.'

Lord Calderstone nodded. If he was surprised by the carefulness of the answer, to what had been largely a social question, he showed no sign of it. Instead he followed the lead which the Captain had opened up.

'She's a big ship, and a fine ship. One of our best. And you've got some good men, I've no doubt. Who's your Staff Commander, by the way?'

'Martin.'

'Oh yes. I remember Martin. He should be a great help to you.'

'I think he will be,' answered Blacklock, 'as soon as we settle down. We've known each other a long time. We were in training ship together.'

'You must be exact contemporaries, then?'

'Just about.'

'I'm sure it will work out,' said Lord Calderstone, who knew all about contemporaries jostling their way to the top of the heap together. He added just enough to make the point. 'Don't forget, when Hope Lines picks a man for captain, they give him all the backing he needs.' Then he looked at his watch. 'Well, well, how quickly the time goes. Only an hour or so, and we shall be off.'

'I hope so,' said the Captain.

Lord Calderstone might have affected surprise, but he did not. 'You mean, you think there's a chance of another hold-up?'

'It's always possible,' said the Captain. 'If it happened yesterday, it can happen today. There's been a lot of talk about the stewards staging something. A sudden walkout – something like that.'

Lord Calderstone nodded again. 'Yes. One of those newspaper chaps was trying to bring it up. He actually asked me what my reaction would be; *if* it happened.' He smiled briefly. 'Sometimes I think the freedom of the press deserves a stronger term altogether ... But there's nothing definite there, is there? No new development?'

'Not that I know of. The trouble is, these things start up out of the blue. One of my stewards is still ashore, seeing McTeague. That could mean something, or it could mean nothing at all.'

'What's the general feeling among the stewards?'

'It's difficult to tell. Most of them seem perfectly happy, and then someone starts talking to them about their grievances, and suddenly they're not happy any longer. Mostly it boils down to McTeague.' Blacklock frowned; he did not feel like disguising his thoughts on this subject. 'Whether this ship sails or not probably depends on that damned barrow boy ashore. I'd like to wring his neck!'

Lord Calderstone raised his eyebrows. 'Oh, I don't know. He's probably not such a bad chap, when you get to know him. Wrong-headed, of course.'

The Captain was far from agreeing, but he said nothing. They both of them knew all about McTeague, from long experience; they knew the tactics he pursued, the sort of hold he had, the number of times he had stopped ships sailing, the number of times he had tried to do so, and just failed, and left a residue of ill will and discontent, for use next time. They both knew he had been a troublemaker, up and down the Liverpool dockside, for many a bitter year. But it was clear that they thought of him in different ways.

Perhaps the difference was the basic difference between Lord Calderstone and the Captain. To Blacklock, McTeague was something like a personal enemy. McTeague tried to stop ships sailing, and tie up shipping lines, and threaten the livelihood of sailors like himself; thus, McTeague was a crook and a bastard, and had to be defeated, if not destroyed. Calderstone, a less vulnerable target, could afford a more urbane view. For him, McTeague was just someone on the other side, and therefore bound to behave as he did; roughly speaking, it was the way he had been brought up, and one shouldn't expect anything better. All one needed to do was to outwit him.

Of course, coming from Lord Calderstone, the term 'wrong-headed' was very strong comment indeed. It was as severe as saying, of someone in his own world, that he was 'not to be taken seriously'. Both brands of eccentric were outside the pale. But Lord Calderstone's approach, and his execution, would be different from the Captain's. If Lord Calderstone had to tackle McTeague, as he was quite ready to do, it would not be on any personal basis; it would be a matter of high principle, an exercise of discipline in the interests of a stable economy.

He made the point himself, with the appropriate gravity, when he went on: 'Of course, I'm not underrating him, nor the importance of what he stands for. For reasons best known to themselves, people like McTeague are never satisfied with what I might call a workable compromise. With them, it's all or nothing – with the "all" going to their side, and the nothing to us.' He smiled, pleased with the turn of phrase. 'I need not tell you how disastrously this can affect the shipping companies, where working costs are paramount, and indeed our whole export trade.' He sat back, comfortably mounted on his favourite topic. 'Exports are vital to us. They are the way of life of this country, the way she earns her bread and pays her way. They are her bloodstream. Stop that bloodstream, or block it in any way, and the heart itself may suffer irreparable damage.'

The Captain had stopped listening – not because he did not agree, but because he did. He knew Calderstone's speech by heart; he had heard it, in a hundred different versions, on a thousand different occasions during the past twenty years. So had everyone else; everyone in Britain knew the vital importance of exports; they had been told about it till they were sick of the very word.

But what they did about it was another matter altogether. The answer, basically, was nothing much. It had become clearer, month by month and year by year, that it would take more than persuasive platitudes about the lifeblood of Old England, to make people see, and act on, this simple truth of survival. With very few exceptions, it would take nothing less than peril, shock, or starvation to get them to work like men.

In common with nearly all sailors, the Captain was an authoritarian. In his view, discussion groups cut no ice;

committees did not reef a ship when a squall struck. One man decided, and the rest did what they were told. They did it in their own interests, as well as those of the man at the top and the owners of the ship. They did it because they knew the facts of life. They knew that if they ever sat about arguing the toss as to whether the reefing were really necessary, or, worse still, demanding to be paid overtime before they climbed the mainmast, they would all be dead men, and from all the argument and the chaffering only bubbles would rise.

To Blacklock, it really did seem as simple as that. It was a matter of discipline. If you wanted something done, you issued the orders, and you punished the disobedient or the slack. On that basis, ships sailed, and came safely to harbour, and sailed again.

He thought about this, and its application to their present danger, until Lord Calderstone seemed to be running out of steam. Then he awoke suddenly to the fact that Lord Calderstone was talking on exactly the same lines.

'That is why,' Lord Calderstone concluded, in a much firmer tone, 'we really cannot go on submitting to this sort of blackmail. We simply cannot afford the risk. In the present case, this ship has to sail, because she has been committed, on a contractual basis involving thousands of people, to doing so.' He looked carefully at the Captain. 'I think it might be prudent to take some precautions.'

The Captain waited.

'The last thing I want to do,' Lord Calderstone went on, with a certain percentage of accuracy, 'is to interfere with your job, or to take a hand in running the show. It's your show, and that's why you're sitting where you are.' He smiled, with great charm. 'However, I am one of your passengers, and I am just as keen as any other passenger that we should get away on time. Speaking purely in that capacity, I do think that we should try to find out a little more about what is going on.'

'About the stewards, you mean?'

'About the stewards. For instance this man who is ashore. What's his name, by the way?'

'Swann.'

'I hope your Swann won't prove to be a goose,' said Lord Calderstone, and waited for the smile which was his due. Then he went on: 'How much backing is he likely to have, if he returns on board with some sort of strike instructions? What percentage of the men are likely to follow him? Would your Chief Steward know about that?'

'Bryce has told me as much as he knows,' answered the Captain. He might have resented this active interference with his command, but in fact he did not; Lord Calderstone and he were on the same side, the alliance of men who wanted the *Good Hope* to sail, and he did not feel he should disdain any supporters nor, for that matter, any advice. 'He thinks that, if McTeague and Swann between them could dream up a solid grievance, about fifty per cent of the catering staff would follow Swann's lead. The rest would be with Tom Renshaw – that's your own steward.'

'Renshaw?' asked Lord Calderstone, surprised. 'How does he come into this?'

'He's the *official* union man, the senior shop steward. Swann is the unofficial spokesman who does all the talking and arguing.'

'That's interesting. That's very interesting indeed … Then Renshaw is likely to know as much as Bryce about all this?'

'More, probably. He's always been close to the men, and he's personally very popular. Even with the young ones, though they don't always listen to his advice, much less take it. I've known him for twenty years,' the Captain went on. 'They call him Uncle Tom. He's the best steward in Hope Lines, I should say.'

'I think I would like to talk to him,' said Lord Calderstone, in sudden decision. 'Here and now. There can be no harm in taking soundings ... But I don't want to make too much of an occasion out of it.'

'I can get him up here,' said the Captain. 'He won't gossip about it.'

'Let's do it another way.' Lord Calderstone felt in his breast pocket, and then in other pockets, with a faintly roguish smile. 'Dear me,' he said, 'I must have left my cigar case in my cabin. Would you be kind enough to send word to my steward to bring it up?'

When the message had been sent, they fell into silence again, the pause before action. Presently the Captain said: 'By the way, Renshaw is Swann's uncle.' Then there was a knock on the door, and Tom Renshaw came in.

In his hand was a silver tray, balanced on the palm, with no intrusive thumb showing; on the tray was a gold cigar case, and the onyx cigar cutter from Lord Calderstone's desk, and a box of matches. It was Hope Lines service at its formal best. Lord Calderstone, with the same sort of ceremonial aplomb, took the case, and from it selected a cigar; snipped off the end, blew gently through it, lit it with great care, puffed five times, removed the band, and sat back in an attitude of contentment, wreathed in the fragrant smoke of a fifteen-shilling *maduro* Montecristo. Then he inclined his head, and said: 'Thank you, Renshaw'.

'Thank you, my Lord.' Tom Renshaw – head erect, back straight, tray in line with the seams of the trousers – turned to go. Lord Calderstone held up his hand, languid yet commanding.

'One moment,' he said. 'I would like to have a word with you.'

Tom Renshaw turned back. 'Certainly, sir.'

'This is in strict confidence. You understand that?'

'Yes, sir.'

Lord Calderstone came straight to the point. 'There's been some talk, which I'm sure you have heard, about dissatisfaction among the stewards. The possibility of a strike, which might hold us up again. Have you anything more to tell us about that?'

Since he had said 'us', Tom Renshaw looked at the Captain, and back again to Lord Calderstone, before he answered. He saw nothing to give him any lead; the Captain's face showed no sign that he was either pleased or displeased at the query. Renshaw therefore took it at its face value; this was the Chairman of the line worrying, as he had every right to do, about the situation aboard one of his ships. He answered confidently: 'There's been nothing worth reporting, sir. Otherwise I'd have told the Chief Steward. I think we'll get away all right. But you can never tell, these days.'

It was a fair answer, but rather too vague and non-committal for Lord Calderstone, who, like all masters of the bromide, did not relish it when administered by other people. With slightly more insistence, he said: 'I want to be able to tell, if possible. Just let me get the picture. You are the senior union representative on board.'

'Yes, sir.'

'The men follow you?'

'Most of them, sir. Of course there's a lot of arguments now and again. But we don't do too badly.'

'You can count on more than half the men, then. A working majority.'

This was coming close to home, and Tom Renshaw's face showed it. He glanced again at the Captain, as if wondering how much it would be safe to say. Still finding no commitment of any sort, he ploughed ahead, a somewhat lonely figure, trying for an honest appraisal.

'I couldn't guarantee that, sir. What I say is – I've had this shop steward job a long time, and mostly things have gone all right. We haven't had a walkout, or anything like that, for near two years. But you can't count on it, not any more. These days, they don't always listen to the union, unless it happens to suit them.'

Lord Calderstone observed the end of his cigar, as if it were some distant object which might or might not prove to be friendly. Then he said: 'They listen to your nephew instead. Is that it?'

Tom Renshaw swallowed. Unfair, his face seemed to say; below the belt; I can't help my nephew ... But he was a steward, and Lord Calderstone, as well as being a lord, was Chairman of the line; he could always get away with that sort of thing. He answered, as stiffly as this branch of the feudal system allowed: 'If you mean young Swann, sir, yes, it's true. A lot of the young lads do listen to him, and follow him. It seems they'll follow anyone that beats the drum. Just now, it's Swann.'

'Or perhaps McTeague.'

'It's the same thing, sir.'

Lord Calderstone stared at him, surprised. 'How do you make that out?'

'I'm afraid they've been pretty thick, the last few months. Nothing I could do about it.' For the third time he glanced at the Captain. 'Matter of fact, sir. Swann's ashore now, seeing McTeague.'

His face, always old and grey, seemed to have taken on a sort of crumpled look; both of the men watching him were struck with the same thought – that it was time to relax the pressure. The Captain said: 'We know that already,' and Lord Calderstone nodded, as if acknowledging something not too much out of the ordinary, not too shameful or embarrassing. There was silence for a brief space, and then

Lord Calderstone took up the questioning again, on the kindest note he had struck so far.

'Tell me about your nephew.'

'Not much to tell, sir.' Tom Renshaw reacted to the tone; it was not him they were after, it was other things, accidents of blood and birth, things he could not help. 'He's a good enough lad in a way, but he's just a silly kid, when it comes to this sort of thing. He's my sister's child. His dad was killed in the war. Since then' – Tom Renshaw shrugged, a human, unstewardly shrug, as if he were explaining some misfortune to friends he could trust – 'I got him this job through Mr Bryce. I thought he'd smarten up, get a bit of lead in his pencil.' He coughed. 'But he never really took to it. He just hasn't got the feeling. He's discontented, like – they all are, these days. He doesn't really believe in anything. And people listen to him, young as he is, because he can put things in a way they understand. And he sings a bit, and plays the guitar in one of those groups.' The unrelated, disjointed picture emerged suddenly as a sharp portrait. 'I don't know where they get their ideas from. They've got them, that's all I know. Or they're ready to pick them up. Like Vic. Soon as he met McTeague, it was like striking a match and chucking it into a gas oven. McTeague talks, and the lad swallows it all whole, and suddenly he feels blown up twice the size of life, and he'll do anything – *anything* – that he thinks McTeague would want. Like he was going out to earn a medal, or something. You can't argue with him. All you can do is to do the best you can, to see he doesn't get away with it.'

Tom Renshaw fell silent. The sketch was completed; he had done better than he knew, in depicting youth in revolt, old age in doubtful misgiving, and a world which seemed to have mislaid the rules of conduct. The Captain felt grateful to him, and sorry for him, and obscurely proud of him; grateful for the honest picture, sorry for Tom Renshaw's entanglement with it, and proud that he had done so well under the searchlight. This was a Hope Lines steward. He would be glad if he himself could do as well, as a Hope Lines captain ... What Lord Calderstone thought of it, however, became more apparent with his next question. Lord Calderstone, a veteran inquisitor, was not going overboard for compassion's sweet sake. He was keeping his head.

'That explains a good deal,' he said, as might a doctor on his hospital rounds, after a brief glance at the temperature chart. 'Of course, it excuses nothing ... Now tell me something about McTeague.'

Tom Renshaw checked a private sigh. He had hoped that they were finished with him; he had talked enough, and bared enough of his secret thoughts, for one day. Now he felt something like resentment; at the beginning, he had been flattered by the confidential inquiry, but the feeling had ebbed to nothing halfway through. It wasn't his job to come up with this sort of report; he was doing the Chief Steward's work for him, and getting precious little thanks in the process. As he hesitated, not too sure how much he wanted to say, or how helpful he wanted to be, Lord Calderstone prompted his answer: 'You've met McTeague, of course.'

'Aye, I've met him.'

'Well, what do you think of him?'

'Not much, sir. He's not my sort. But I can understand what he's after.'

'Can you, indeed?'

'Yes, sir,' said Tom Renshaw, with a shade of extra promptness. They wanted to hear about McTeague? – well, let them hear ... 'He likes to stir up trouble, because he's had nothing but trouble all his life. He's another one you can't argue with. He's had a hard life, and he wants to pay back for it.'

'Is that so?' said Lord Calderstone, austerely. 'What a very strange world it would be, if we all behaved like that. And what exactly has this so-called "hard life" involved?'

Tom Renshaw was not daunted. 'You remember the thirties, sir?'

'Of course.'

'Well, McTeague was a Liverpool lad in the thirties. His dad was out of work for years. So was he. I'm not saying they starved – '

'No one starved,' said Lord Calderstone.

'There was a good few went hungry.'

Lord Calderstone gave him a swift whose-side-are-you-on look, and then softened it with a gentler nodding of the head. 'They were very hard times,' he said. 'I'm not denying it. Some of my own companies had a very tricky time, before we turned the corner. But that was thirty years ago. Things have improved vastly since then. Surely the effect cannot last so long, when so many of the problems have disappeared altogether. And what about your own case? You were a young man then, weren't you? You must have gone through the same hard times, suffered the same hardships.'

'Aye,' said Renshaw. 'We all did.'

'Yet you have obviously turned out very different from McTeague.'

Tom Renshaw gave a slight shrug. 'Reckon he must have been hit harder, sir. I'm not excusing him, any road. Him and me are on opposite sides, all right. And we got him off the executive, double quick, when we saw the way things were going. But like I said, you can see what he's after, and you can see why.'

'What he is after, in fact, is industrial unrest, indefinitely prolonged.'

Tom Renshaw supplied his own translation. 'He'd like to stop the ship, sir. This ship, and any other ship. He's been doing it for years.'

'But where does it get him?'

'It makes him feel better.'

The homely phrase seemed to hang in the still air of the cabin, explaining much, comforting not at all. Lord Calderstone, silent and thoughtful, was gazing at a drift of cigar smoke; the Captain, watching Tom Renshaw, was pondering one of his phrases – how one man could be 'harder hit' than another, how hatred could gorge and bloat upon itself forever, how certain wounds could never heal ... He could not remember the thirties himself, save as a time of worried faces at home, and occasional talk – not too censorious – about the Liverpool mounted police wading into unemployed demonstrations, over on the Birkenhead side. His own baptism of fire had been wartime convoys, as a twenty-year-old fourth mate, and that, for one reason or another, had been a lot easier ... He came out of his small daydream to find Lord Calderstone, who could close any meeting in any one of a dozen different keys, in process of ending this session, without undue delay, on his own particular note of infinitely polite detachment.

'I think we might perhaps leave it there,' he said, to the world at large. And then, to Tom Renshaw: 'I won't be changing for dinner, of course. I'll have my bath at half past six.'

'Very good, sir,' said Renshaw.

'And a clean shirt, please.'

'Yes, my lord.'

'And thank you, Renshaw. You have really been a great help.'

The door closed behind him. With the briefest possible pause, Lord Calderstone spoke again.

'A good man,' he said. 'A first-class man. Perhaps a trifle lacking in firmness, having regard to his position in the union. But one cannot expect everything.'

'He's a good man, all right,' said the Captain.

'Quite so ...' Lord Calderstone drew on his cigar, and then said, suddenly and flatly: 'I don't like the sound of this at all.'

It was almost as if another man had spoken. The impeccable tone and outlook, the easy, proper-way-to-treat-a-servant manner had evaporated; a page had been turned, and the next one belonged to a different book altogether. It was clear that what had been appropriate for the session with Tom Renshaw now fell short of requirements, and must be changed. That much was understandable. But it still surprised the Captain that Lord Calderstone could effect the change so swiftly and smoothly, as if he had only to flick a switch on some internal, automatic salad bowl of behaviour, and alter the setting from bland to raw.

The Captain himself was more at home with the new man than the old. 'I don't like the sound of it, either. It's the same old pattern. Seems we're plagued like this, almost every voyage. We had exactly the same trouble, last year in the *Grand*.'

'But the *Grand Hope* sailed, I remember.'

'In the end, yes.'

'Quite so. And that is what this ship is going to do now.' Lord Calderstone tapped his fingers on the arm of his chair, by way of emphasis; with his next words, it became clear that the small gesture reflected massive determination. 'We *will* sail! I simply will not tolerate this sort of thing any longer.'

He was staring directly at the Captain, and suddenly he was much less charming, much less of a fourth baron, much more of a top-level executive with profits in peril.

He looked, the Captain realized, exactly what he was: a tough, shrewd, and durable man who happened to have been born with a title. That was why he was sitting in that chair at that particular moment; he was head of Hope Lines because he had earned it, along with all the rest; a lesser man – a title with a gap underneath it – might have been shouldered aside long ago. But Calderstone had reached the top, like any other climber – like the Captain himself; and he was aiming to stay there. That, once again, made them two of a kind.

Now Calderstone was talking, for the second time, about exports. But this time they sounded different, they sounded real.

'This ship is going to get away today,' said Lord Calderstone, 'because I want her to, and you certainly want her to, and in the last analysis, England wants her to.' It did not sound pompous, or even oratorical; it sounded straightforward and reasonable. 'You know me as the Chairman of Hope Lines,' he went on. 'I may add that I hold forty-four other directorships, and many of them are closely involved with this ship. One of them is the bank which financed her building – a bank which expects a regular return on its outlay. Another makes the paint which keeps her looking smart. You have twenty-two of our cars – special export models – in Number Four hold. You have two thousand cases of *my* Scotch whisky. There is a 36 ton piece of hydro-electric machinery in Number Three. It comes from one of our foundries. These – and there are lots of others – are the sort of things that England depends on, simply to make a living.' He paused; not for effect – though he had an effect – but for his summing-up. 'That being so,' said Lord Calderstone, 'I am damned if anyone, whatever his motives, is going to stop this cargo getting to New York, or stop the cruise that comes directly afterwards, or stop anything that concerns the *Good Hope*.

In the general interest, this ship has to sail by six o'clock. And that's all there is to it.'

The Captain might have added one more item, dearest of all to his heart: that the *Good Hope's* voyage was part of a regular passenger schedule, that he had embarked five hundred passengers who, counting on this, had already been held up for twenty-four hours; and that, rich or poor, landed gentry or common as dirt, they were all parties to a fair bargain and were entitled to have it honoured. But he let it go. Lord Calderstone had made out his case, and it was a good one, a case not to be quarrelled with; it only remained to see that it went through.

He said: 'Of course, I'm with you there, sir.' It seemed an appropriate moment to add the 'sir'; indeed, it was the first time he had really wanted to. 'It's essential that we get away tonight. The trouble is, it's not really in our hands, is it?'

Lord Calderstone, still very much in the driver's seat, gave him a cold glance. 'Then the sooner we get it into our hands, the better. This is a crisis, or it seems likely to become one. It is not of our choosing, but it is there, just the same. We must therefore find some way of meeting it, if necessary head-on.'

The Captain opened his mouth to say: At the moment there's nothing to meet, either head-on or back to back. But suddenly there was something to meet; and its onset only needed three swift steps: a knock on the cabin door, the entrance of Staff Commander Martin, and his first foreboding words: 'Excuse me, sir. Can I see you urgently?'

He had spoken to the Captain, but immediately his eyes shifted to Lord Calderstone; it was apparent that, if this were to prove to be his big scene, Staff Commander Martin would be playing it to the Chairman. The Captain surveyed him with all the dislike customarily reserved for bearers of bad news, plus a personal dividend grounded in something else: the suspicion that Martin was a conniving bastard who would somehow turn this thing – whatever it was – to his own advantage. His voice as he answered was very curt.

'What is it, Staff?'

With reluctance, Martin faced the Captain again. 'Sir,' he said manfully, 'you told me to report any new developments about the situation with the stewards. I'm afraid that I have something to report.'

He paused. His timing would have done credit to many an actor on a far wider stage, and the Captain, already irritated, felt ready to explode. If they had been alone, he would have snapped: 'Get on with it, then!' But he was beginning to realize that his new status did not allow such luxuries. Instead he said: 'Well?'

'Sir, you told me to have Swann logged as soon as he came back on board.' Martin turned courteously to Lord Calderstone. 'Perhaps I should explain that Swann is one of our Tourist stewards. He – '

'I know all about Swann,' said Lord Calderstone, and the Captain blessed him for it. 'Just tell us what he has been doing.'

Martin collected himself. 'Following your instructions' – the repeated emphasis sounded an early alarm system in the Captain's brain, but he could only wait to see how it would be followed through – 'I left orders for Swann to report to the Chief Steward as soon as he came on board. He did not do so. Instead he just lounged about, not answering his bells, generally playing the fool. Finally he was reported to me, and I – ah – had to take action.'

They waited for another short, meaningful pause. 'In the circumstances,' said Martin earnestly, 'and with things being so tricky, I might just have given him a rocket, and let it go at that. But you did give me the impression, sir' – he was speaking very deliberately, with, the Captain realized, a careful economy of truth – 'that he was not to be allowed to get away with anything. So, as I said, I had to discipline him.'

'How did you discipline him?'

'I took him off the Tourist roster, and assigned him to the junior officers' mess.'

The Captain almost winced. Waiting on the junior officers, a noisy, bumptious, and penniless lot, was for obvious reasons the most unpopular job on board; it was given to newly recruited catering staff or, in a few cases, to very old stewards who could not really pull their weight in any other part of the ship. It was immediately obvious that Martin had handled the matter of Swann with the minimum of tact. There was nothing that one could really pin down, and, as his phrasing made clear, he was covering himself well, when it came to assigning the blame. It was just that, at this crucial moment, he had decided not to give any help.

Lord Calderstone broke the silence. 'How did Swann take it?'

'He was grossly insubordinate,' answered Martin, with a certain relish. 'In fact, seeing his attitude, I was very glad that I had – er – followed the Captain's orders. First he said that I couldn't do this to him. Then he said he would refuse the duty. Finally he said something like "We'll see about this", and practically ran out of my cabin. I'm very much afraid, sir, that he's probably holding his protest meeting now.'

The Captain came to life. He said, almost ferociously: 'Thank you, Staff. That'll do for now.'

An injured look came into Martin's face, as if he were being robbed of the meatiest part of his role, upstaged by a rank amateur. 'If you want me to take any further action' – he began.

'I do not,' said the Captain, and pointed a decisive finger towards the door.

When Martin had gone, Lord Calderstone said, surprisingly: 'I see what you mean,' and then: 'Now – let's take a fresh look at all this.'

He began to talk briskly; but, once again, the Captain scarcely heard him. If he was listening to anything, it was his own murderous thoughts. Martin had let him down, with a vindictive bump; he could not have devised a form of discipline more likely to catch Swann on the raw, and ensure a swift reaction. Furthermore, he had managed to convey the impression, vital for the future, that the whole thing had flowered from some stupid insistence, on the part of the Captain, that rules were rules and had to be enforced, whatever the circumstances, whatever the cost.

Even if Lord Calderstone had not been fooled, Martin had gone a long way towards clearing his yardarm. In any case, all the grisly facts remained. They had a first-class row on their hands, brought to its crux by a man who should have been a useful ally and had proved himself a rat; they stood on the edge of failure, and there was damned little time to do anything about it.

This, it seemed, was what Lord Calderstone was now saying, in phrases whose smoothness did not disguise the same sort of edge. He was glancing at his watch.

'We have little more than an hour,' he said. 'We really cannot await Swann's convenience, until he decides whether or not to lead the men out. If we are going to sail, we must take the initiative.' He looked at the Captain. 'I fully realize your difficulties, Blacklock. But in matters like this there comes a moment – '

Pressure, thought the Captain morosely; I'm just about fed up with pressure ... It seemed as if he were being jabbed at from a dozen different angles, by a dozen different arguments and claims; he was the focus of every sort of wrangling persuasion – from people like Swann, from people like Martin, from people like Lord Calderstone, from his innocent passengers, and above all from his own professional sense, which was outraged by this disorder.

'I think we would be justified' – Lord Calderstone was saying, when the Captain cut him short. It was the word 'we' which finally sparked his rebellion. It wasn't a matter of 'we', at all: whatever his allies, whatever his enemies and faint-hearted friends, he stood alone, and the job was his, and no one else's. Now was the time to show it, in unmistakable terms. Otherwise, he would never feel like a captain again.

'I'll sort this out myself,' he said, so suddenly and loudly that Lord Calderstone blinked. But Calderstone did not try to speak again; there was no need to; it was not that sort of moment. He watched, with pleasure and some surprise, as the Captain pressed a bell, and his steward answered, at a pace which stewards could always muster when they had been eavesdropping on critical events.

'Find the Chief Steward,' the Captain told him. 'Tell him, from me, to bring Steward Swann up to my cabin. Whatever he's doing.' And as that man hesitated, not fully up-to-date with history: 'Now!' the Captain barked out, in a voice which might have been heard from the bridge to the foc's'le. 'And get going! I haven't got all day.'

In the silence that followed, the Captain glanced up at the clock on the wall, and saw how truly he had spoken. He had indeed not got all day. It was five o'clock, and whatever he had to do, there was a bare hour left to do it in.

CHAPTER FOUR

The Man of the Moment

❖

It was just after four o'clock, and growing towards a gloomy winter dusk, when Victor Winston Swann returned on board the *Good Hope*. But he scarcely saw the gloom, nor the grimy wet planking he trod; he was in a sunshine mood, a mood of prime self-confidence. At last, something worthwhile had been put on his plate ... He was tremendously aware of himself as the trusted emissary from the government-in-exile, the man they were all depending on. He had been given a big job, a real job, the best job in Liverpool that day; and as he moved down the quay, and drew near the towering white bulk of the *Good Hope*, he knew he could bring it off. Big as she was, one man could tie her up single-handed, if he put his mind to it. It only needed a fair chance, and a little fancy footwork, and a bit of luck.

The ship looked trim, and smart, and ready to sail; but that was all a lot of eyewash. She was not going to sail; she was going to stay right where she was.

He sauntered up the stern gangway, whistling the same tune – '*Wish me luck, as you wave me goodbye*' – with which he had said farewell to McTeague. His manner was jaunty;

and it did not grow less jaunty when, at the top of the gangway, the Master-at-Arms placed a large, flat hand against his chest, and growled: 'Just a minute, you. I've got some orders for you.'

Swann grinned cockily. 'Don't tell me. I'm under arrest.' He backed away from the detaining hand, as if it were something he did not care to associate with, and leant against the nearest bulkhead. 'You better be careful who you're pushing, all the same. You shove me about, I can have you up for assault.'

The other man surveyed him with grim dislike. 'Steward Swann. Report to the Chief Steward. And don't forget I told you.'

'Okey-doke.'

'You're to report now,' said the Master-at-Arms, who was of a different generation, and glad of it. 'So just you hop to it.'

'Master, I hear and obey.'

But he did not obey. There was plenty of time for that; he was heading into trouble, as it was – trouble which would lead him to the Chief Steward, and maybe a long way beyond, in any case. He needn't do anything he didn't have a liking for ... He gave the Master-at-Arms a low, derisive bow, and began to dawdle his way forward in the direction of the Tourist cabins.

Many of them were empty. It was very much the off-season now, and the promise of eight days in the wintry North Atlantic could hardly compete with a six-hour, rock-steady, weatherless crossing by jet plane. The *Good Hope* would only wake up properly at New York, when a gang of rich old loafers tottered on board for a month's boozing it up in the Caribbean ... But here and there were pockets of activity; children running up and down the passages, people saying goodbye, stewards knocking on doors and bringing in last-minute parcels. Near at hand, a bell was ringing, insistently, bad-temperedly. It was probably ringing for him. Let it ring.

Swann took a right turn down an alleyway, and into a section of cabins reserved for women travelling by themselves. He had no business to be there; by company regulations, all the attendance in this section was provided by stewardesses. But he was not in the mood to watch the regulations. He was his own man, this afternoon; he was looking for trouble, and, in the meantime, it would do no harm to take a look at the girls.

He was quickly rewarded. Through an open cabin door he caught sight of a girl – or rather, the small slim back of a girl, bending over something on the floor. He took in the picture, unhurriedly. The angle was a shapely and promising one, the skirt nice and tight. It was easy to imagine that she was having trouble with something. He walked quickly forward.

'Can I help you?'

'Oh.' The girl straightened up suddenly, and turned, brushing the hair out of her eyes. He had struck lucky, first time; she was pretty and dark, with a lively face and a pair of pert little breasts pushing energetically out from her sweater. 'You know, you made me jump.'

Vic Swann smiled. I'll make you jump, he thought; jump right off the mattress. 'Thought you might need some help.' She had been bending over a suitcase, and he transferred his eyes, not too promptly, to this. 'Can't you open it, or something?'

She looked at him inquiringly. Wearing his raincoat, he might have been anyone. But he was young, and nice-looking; the first likely one she had seen on board. Everyone else was so old ... She said: 'Well, if you *could* ... The lock's stuck, I think. D'you know anything about locks?'

'I know a bit about everything,' said Swann, with another smile. He knelt down, applied a firm thumb to the catch, and the lock sprang back. 'See – one wave of my magic wand.' Still on his knees, he looked up and asked: 'Want me to open the lid for you?'

'You just leave it be,' said the girl, with the right touch of flirtatiousness. 'You might see some of my secrets.'

Swann stood up, and backed away a little, till he was leaning in the doorway. She really was pretty, just ripe for it. Her cabin was for two people, and the other berth already had a suitcase on it. But that needn't make any difference. There were all sorts of ways, with two, even three girls to a cabin. Sometimes all it meant was, they quarrelled about whose turn it was. The sea did something to girls, and thank God for it.

'You can't shock me,' said Swann. 'But you can always try ... Is this your first trip over?'

'Yes. Isn't it lovely?'

'I've done too many,' said Swann, the man of the world. 'But yes, from here it looks lovely.'

The girl tossed her head, not at all put out. 'I can see I'll have to keep my eye on you. How many trips have you done?'

'It's about my twenty-first,' said Swann. 'Professionally, that is. You see, this is my ship. I work on board.'

'Ooh.' She was impressed, and she widened her eyes to show it. 'Are you an officer?'

'Sort of.'

'My mum said to be careful of the officers. She said sailors are terribly romantic.'

'Then we'll get on all right, won't we? What's your name?'

'Freda.'

'That's a pretty one. Pretty name for the prettiest girl on board. And I bet you are, too.'

'Have you seen all the others, then?'

'I don't have to.'

'Well, you're not shy, I'll say that. My mum must have been right, after all.' She sighed. 'I'm going to America. Emigrating.'

'All on your lonesome, eh?'

'Yes. I'm going to be a nurse.'

'In a hospital?' This was looking better and better. Nurses were guaranteed to be hot stuff. They had to know all about it – part of the training.

'No. In a family. Children's nurse.'

'Oh.' No better than a servant, thought Swann. But she was pretty, all right. Perhaps the *Good Hope* had better sail after all. In a few days ... He said: 'I can just see you with a lot of kids.'

She giggled. 'Give me time ... What's your name?' She eyed his hair. 'Curly?'

'Vic. Vic Swann.'

An echo from behind him, on a much harsher note, suddenly called out: '*Swann!*'

Swann could not help jumping, though he would have given a lot of money not to; the contrast between the small idyll in the cabin, and the hard voice of authority from outside, was as embarrassing as it could possibly be. The interrupter was the Chief Steward, of course, standing in the alleyway, glaring at him; and the girl, who was as startled as he, could see that Bryce was glaring, and had heard the tone of the voice, and must be adding two and two together and making a damned silly sum out of it ... Swann said, with a brave grin: 'Excuse me a minute,' and backed out of the cabin, shutting the door behind him. Then, ashamed and angry, he turned to face the newcomer.

Chief Steward Bryce was angry too. 'What the hell are you doing here?' he asked loudly. 'You know the regulations. What are you up to?'

'I was helping her with her suitcase,' said Swann sulkily. He sought to move down the alleyway, because the girl must be able to hear every word, but Bryce barred his way, just by standing there.

'There's a stewardess to do that,' said Bryce. 'You've no call to help her with anything. You've got your own work, and it's about time you got down to it.' The loud, hectoring tone seemed to ring up and down the corridors. 'Weren't you told to report to me?'

'I was on my way.' Swann was beginning to recover from the surprise, and with recovery came a return of spirit. 'Had to make a bit of a detour, like. Can't be in two places at once, can I?'

'You've been on board nearly ten minutes,' said Bryce. 'It doesn't take you ten minutes to get from the stern gangway to my office.' His voice grew easier, almost genial. 'You know, you're going to be in big trouble if you carry on like this. You're logged, anyway. Staff Commander's report, tomorrow morning.'

'OK.'

'And talk properly, for Christ's sake! You sound like a snotty little schoolkid.'

'Oh, leave me alone.' Swann pushed past him, not caring how much force he used, and Bryce had to give way. 'You're always after me for something. It's victimization, that's what it is.'

'Come off it! I'm after you because you don't do your work, and well you know it.' And as Swann seemed to be walking away: 'Just a minute,' said the Chief Steward. 'I haven't finished with you yet.'

'What is it now, then?'

'Your bell's been ringing for five minutes or more. Cabin B19. Why hasn't it been answered?'

'I was told to report to you,' answered Swann cheekily. 'I can't answer bells at the same time, can I?'

'Then what were you lounging about here for?'

'My job's to make the passengers comfortable,' said Swann with a smirk. 'You're always on to us about that. I see a young lady wants her suitcase unlocked, I don't hang about doing nothing. I volunteer for the job. And very nice too. Another satisfied customer.'

'She can ring for the stewardess. Or you can.'

'Thought I'd save us both a bit of trouble.' Swann sighed, theatrically. 'Seems like I can't get anything right today.'

Bryce jerked his head towards the closed cabin door. 'You leave passengers like her alone, or you'll be in real trouble yourself.' He surveyed Swann with active distaste. 'Now just get this straight. You've been logged once already today. If you go on like this, you'll finish up in the clink, and that's a promise. I've had all the sauce I want from you, my lad. Now get back to your pantry, and take that coat off, and answer the bell in B19.'

'I want to go to the lavatory,' said Swann. 'Can I do that too?'

'Stop fooling about!'

'Sorry. I thought maybe I had to get permission.'

'Get on with it, Swann.'

'Yes, sir!' Swann turned, and walked down the alleyway. At the corner, he began to whistle again, and then to laugh to himself. His spirits lifted as he walked. The girl wasn't important. The job for McTeague was. And that seemed to have started very well indeed.

Cabin B19 was a mean little slit of a place, an 'inside' room about as far from the sea as it could possibly be, unstrategically placed between the drying room and the back of the Tourist bar; it was probably the cheapest single cabin in the ship. Designed in more spacious days, for someone's chauffeur or valet, it now did duty, under the heading 'Minimum Tourist Accommodation' for those passengers whose aim was to cross the Atlantic and still have their pennies to count at the other end.

Swann had looked after it for some six months; he gave it the attention he thought it deserved, which in turn was related to the ten-shilling tip he would be lucky to get at the end of the voyage. For one reason or another, the bell did not often ring in B19.

Today was an exception, as the green telltale light over the door showed. Swann reached up to switch it out again, and then knocked on the door, wondering what he would find on the other side. He had been ashore when the occupant arrived; all he knew was the name, 'Ogilvie, Mr C.', which was on the cabin plan. Probably another of those penny-pinching Scotch immigrants, wolfing oats like a horse and bawling away at 'Annie Laurie' round the Tourist bar piano at two o'clock in the morning ... He knocked again, since the first call had not been answered, and this time a voice called impatiently: 'Come in, come in.'

It was an unexpected voice, cultured and precise – 'Lah-di-dah' was how Swann classified it, straight away, and the unexpected man it belonged to was also lah-di-dah. He was an old man, very small, very neat, very spruce, wearing a monocle with a thin purple ribbon attached to it – a ribbon which wandered negligently across an elegant frilled shirtfront. His small pointed shoes, though worn and cracked, shone brilliantly; his white hair was meticulously combed. He was sitting on the edge of his bunk, with a pad on his knee and his feet on a suitcase, writing; and he did not look up as the door opened.

'Were you ringing?' asked Swann. He did not like little old men putting on airs in cabins like B19, and his voice showed it.

The old man carefully completed the sentence he was engaged on, and then raised his head. His face was yellow and wrinkled, with fiery little tufted eyebrows sprouting out like questing antennae. At the moment, the eyebrows looked angry; and indeed Mr C. Ogilvie, it seemed, was himself in a very bad humour.

'Yes,' he said, in a small dry voice. 'I *was* ringing. And the bell was answered – eventually. I wanted some notepaper. A stewardess had to bring me some. Unless your standards have dropped *abysmally* since I last travelled with Hope Lines, there should be a supply of notepaper in each cabin.'

He was looking at Swann as if he personally were the culprit, and a small scruffy culprit at that. This is all I need today, thought Swann, between anger and anticipation; a silly old man talking like this, chucking his weight about, in B19. He did not answer, waiting for it all to happen. He could even see that the process would be swift.

After a moment, Mr Ogilvie said: 'Are you my proper steward?'

Swann nodded, his hands on his hips. 'That's right.'

'I do not like being kept waiting. I had some important letters to write before the mail closed. Now I may not be able to complete them in time.'

'There's a writing room,' said Swann. 'You could have gone there.'

'I am fully aware that there is a public writing room,' answered Mr Ogilvie tartly. 'I happened to want to write my letters in privacy.' He was glaring at Swann, his eyebrows positively bristling. 'Don't they teach you to say "sir" on board this ship?'

'Sometimes,' said Swann. 'It's all according.'

'I am Mr Ogilvie,' said the old man. 'Mr *Charles* Ogilvie. I am not accustomed to this sort of treatment. If you and I are going to get along – '

'P'raps we won't.'

'Pray, what do you mean by that?'

'Well, you never know how things'll work out, do you?'

'Don't be impertinent! I will not be subjected to this sort of behaviour. You call yourself a steward? I very much doubt if you have earned any right to the title!'

'This is the Tourist,' said Swann. 'Not Buckingham Palace.' He waved a hand round the cramped little cabin. 'Know what I mean?'

'I believe that I do,' said Mr Ogilvie. He was beginning to tremble; his monocle fell, and dangled at the end of its purple ribbon. 'And let me tell you, I will not tolerate it for a single moment! I expect the same standards of service – '

'Is there anything else you want?' Swann interrupted roughly.

'No, there is not! Except to report you for the most monstrous impertinence!' Then he remembered something, and corrected himself angrily. 'Yes, I did ring again. I require some stamps.'

'Well, make your mind up.'

'Hold your tongue! I want four threepenny stamps.'

'That's at the bureau,' said Swann.

'What do you mean by that?'

'Stamps. They're on sale at the Purser's bureau.' He added, cruelly: 'Cash only.'

Mr Ogilvie rose to his feet. He was not more than five feet tall, and his body was small and shrunken; yet he seemed to be swelling with anger, as if he might strike Swann down then and there.

'For that, I will report you immediately,' he stuttered. 'What is your name?'

Swann pointed to the small card by the door. 'It's written up there.'

'*What is your name?*'

'Use your eyeglass,' said Swann crudely. 'And then shove it up, for all I care.'

He slammed the door after him. The cabin bell began to ring even as he did so, and its shrill tone followed him as he walked down the passageway, grinning broadly. This was it, this was just what he had been looking for. In fact, it was perfect.

Ten minutes later he was standing in Bryce's office, face to face with a scandalized Chief Steward. Uncle Tom Renshaw was there also, on the other side of the desk; hurriedly summoned, Swann guessed, to witness what might turn into a first-class union row. The atmosphere was already sulphurous when Swann arrived, and it did not get any better as he answered the questions they fired at him.

But once again, it all worked out easy; it seemed that he had only to walk through his role, supplying the answers according to the mood he was in, for everything to move another step towards the very thing that he, and McTeague behind him, were aiming at.

'Seems like you've done it again,' said Chief Steward Bryce, as soon as the door was closed. 'I gave you warning, didn't I? But you wouldn't take it ... What was it you said to Mr Ogilvie?'

Swann was relaxed. *They* had the troubles, not him. 'Who's he when he's at home?'

'You know who he is, all right. Cabin B19.'

'Oh, him.' Swann grinned. 'Proper little comic, isn't he? Like Danny Kaye, only a hundred years old. I *liked* him!'

Uncle Tom, watching him with an embarrassed frown, said: 'Come off it, Vic. This is serious. Answer the Chief Steward properly.'

They waited.

'I didn't say anything to him, that I know of,' Swann volunteered finally. 'He wanted me to fetch him some stamps. I said he should buy them at the bureau. That's fair enough, isn't it?'

'Why didn't you get them for him?'

'What – out of my own money? Why should I?'

'Cut it out,' snapped Bryce. 'Of course he would have paid for them.'

'How was I to know that? He looked like he didn't have the price of a tram ticket.'

'He's a passenger,' said Uncle Tom sharply.

'He's in B19. Millionaire's Row – I don't think!'

'That's not the point, anyway,' cut in Bryce. 'He claims you were rude to him. "Offensive and insolent" was what he said. He's made a formal complaint about it. It's got to go to the Staff Commander, unless you can satisfy me about it. So let's hear your side. *Were* you rude to him?'

Swann considered. 'I told him off a bit, yes.'

'Told him off?' Bryce's voice was incredulous. 'What d'you mean, told him off? Since when have you been telling off the passengers?'

'He started it,' said Swann. 'He's got no call to send me running errands like that.'

Uncle Tom spoke again, in the same tone as Bryce. 'But that's what you're there for! What's wrong with you? You better buck your ideas up a bit! You're getting too big for your boots, and that's the truth ... Anyway, he's an old man, old enough to be your granddad. You ought to be ashamed of yourself! If he wants you to fetch something, you just fetch it for him. It won't break your heart to do a bit of work for a change.'

'I'm not going round buying stamps for any passenger that tells me,' said Vic Swann stubbornly. 'Laying out my own money, with a fat chance of getting it back again! There's nothing in the regulations about that.'

'You were rude to him,' said Bryce, with equal determination. 'You said so yourself. There's no excuse for that, and you know it.'

'I was rude to him because he asked for it. Putting on airs ... Who does he think he is? I know his sort. Come down in the world, and won't admit it. I bet I make more in a week than he does in a month ... But he won't face it. Spends fifty quid on a cabin like B19, and expects to be treated like Lord Bloody Calderstone, with a few extra knobs on. Well, he won't get any soft soap from me, and that's a fact!'

'You're meant to look after the passengers,' said Uncle Tom. 'It's your job.'

'I'll look after them,' said Swann. 'And I'll see they don't chuck their weight about, either. They're just a lot of cheap layabouts, that's all they are! And as soon as they come aboard they expect to be waited on hand and foot.' He mimicked Mr Ogilvie's precise voice. 'Are you my proper steward? You'd think they had fifty footmen and butlers and God knows what – all waiting on them at home. Lots of them, this is the first time they ever saw a bell, or had a chance to ring it. I tell you, I'm not buying stamps for the likes of old man Ogilvie, and there's not a law in the land that can make me.'

'You didn't have to be rude to him,' said Bryce. 'You can't get past that.'

'I don't have to get past it. I was fed up, that's all. And so would you have been, if you'd seen him sitting there like God Almighty, waiting for someone to tell him the time of day. Passengers!' Swann almost spat out the word. 'They're a load of old rubbish, that's what! I'd as soon wait on a bunch of pigs! But they're not putting anything over on me!'

Now there was a pause, and it was, Swann quickly realized, a dangerous pause, from his point of view. He had made out a case, almost from force of habit, and it had stopped them cold. Bryce was sitting there, bad-tempered, violently disapproving, yet speechless; old Uncle Tom was the same. This was the moment when it could go either way; he was in actual danger of getting away with it – they might just tell him to be a better boy next time, and that would be the end of it.

There was another reason why they were sitting there like ducks in a thunderstorm. They didn't know what to say next, because they were afraid; afraid of a real row, afraid of a walkout, afraid of upsetting the whole apple cart. With less than an hour to go, and the ship just ready to sail, they weren't going to risk anything. There was a chance that his whole scheme might come to nothing ... Swann squared his shoulders. He had to change his tactics, and do it very soon; otherwise Bryce would say something like: 'I'm going to warn you once more,' and give him a lecture, and the *Good Hope* would be off in time, full of happy stewards.

Invisibly, determinedly, he took a fresh grip of the handle, and made ready for one more decisive swing.

'Anyway,' he said coolly, 'I've got a complaint of my own to make. You bringing me up here on a false charge, making out I'm some sort of criminal. It's victimization, that's what it is. The lads don't like it, and I don't like it, either.' He looked sullenly at the Chief Steward. 'Just tell me why you're always picking on me. That's what I want to know.'

'Picking on you!' Bryce, who might have been ready for some sort of accommodation, now fairly exploded. 'Let me tell you, I've let you get away with more than anyone else on this ship! Maybe that's what the trouble is. You're lazy, you're workshy, you're impudent, and you're a bloody nuisance! Picking on you? You're damned lucky you've still got a job on board!'

'I don't want to be lucky,' said Swann. 'You aiming to get me the sack? Just try it, that's all! You've been after me for months, haven't you? Anything'll do, so long as you can raise a row about it. Well, it's going to stop. I've got my rights, and I've had enough of being shoved about by the likes of you. You know what you are? You're just a stooge for the officers, that's all. You suck up to them, and you snoop around us, and that's all your job is. What a way to make a living! I'd rather jump in the lavat'ry and pull the chain. If you heard what some of the lads say about you – '

He had aimed to spark a final crisis, and when it came it was a swift one.

'That's enough from you,' said Bryce curtly. He had risen to his feet; he was coldly angry now, no longer doubtful of how to deal with it. Tom Renshaw, shaking his head, watched him as he went into action; but he could do nothing to stand in his way, nor did he want to. 'That's it, Swann. You come along with me to the Staff Commander. He'll soon sort this out.'

Swann grinned cheekily. It might be the last cheeky grin of that day, but it was worth it. 'Why the Staff? Can't you handle it yourself?'

'I can handle it,' said Bryce grimly. 'And so can the Staff Commander. By the time he's finished with you, my lad, you'll be sorry you ever started this lark.'

'*You* started it,' said Swann. 'Or old man Ogilvie started it. Or maybe even Uncle Tom started it. I didn't start it – that's all I know. But let's see how it finishes up, eh?'

When at last he was brought into the Captain's cabin, Swann was in a genuinely bad temper, with no need to dress up his resentment bigger and blacker than it was. The collision with the Staff Commander had given him just the sort of grievance he wanted; but no sooner had his protest meeting got underway, and going nicely, than he was yanked out of it by Bryce, backed up by a stern-jawed Master-at-Arms who was observed to be smiling slightly, for the first time within living memory. The interruption had brought some energetic protests; boos and catcalls had followed their exit; but the meeting had come to a dead stop all the same, and he knew that it would never start up again until he returned.

The lads needed a leader, particularly at a moment like this; and he was the man they needed, and no one else would do. That was what made it so infuriating, to be pulled out just when things were starting to swim.

Yet behind the bad temper was a wary watchfulness. Whatever happened here was only another step, but it was likely to be the final step, the one that really counted; and he was no longer dealing with nobodies. Swann had never thought much of Captain Blacklock, nor of any other captain – 'Pocket Hitlers' was his favourite phrase, where they were concerned, and he used it on all possible occasions; but he could not deny that some sort of halo surrounded them, when they were on board.

They could do all sorts of funny things, things that ordinary people couldn't, and no questions would be asked. It was tied up with the Articles of Agreement you signed when you were taken on; they could really nail a man down, unless he watched out for himself. Maybe McTeague should take a look into that, too … Meanwhile, he would just have to go carefully, like he had been told; get the interview over quickly, go back to his meeting, and liven it up enough to clinch the walkout.

The Captain was less sure of himself than he looked. He sat four-square behind his desk, staring at the two figures as they entered his cabin; Bryce, tall and thin, sharp-faced, stepping like a prison warder who has foiled one escape and is on the lookout for the next one; and Swann, small, determined, keeping his eyes open, keeping his head in surroundings which had often daunted lesser transgressors. The Captain had sent for him, almost on an impulse; the impulse was to do something – anything – which would clear the air, catch up with the odds, and put the *Good Hope* in a position to make her tide.

He really had no idea how he was going to handle it, nor if it were going to work; he only knew that nothing else was going to work – not optimism, not delay, not the blind eye of cowed authority, not waiting to see who struck the first blow, and from what angle. This young idler – he was surveying Swann with a frosty eye, wondering how such an obvious little squirt could ever lead anything bigger than a cinema queue – was in a position to ruin a thousand legitimate hopes; and faced with this the Captain had followed an ingrained sailor's instinct – to grapple the enemy, and see what grappling would bring.

He should perhaps have had the Staff Commander there as well, to complete the chain of authority; but he had had enough of the Staff Commander for that day. He wanted only staunch allies, and if no allies, then himself alone. The fact that Lord Calderstone, an undoubted supporter, had withdrawn into the background, standing by one of the portholes as if divided between the view outside and the vulgar tug-of-war within, did not worry him. He had a feeling that from now on it was to be sailor's work, or none at all.

But it had to be quick work, in any case. The time was ten past five.

The preliminaries were easy enough.

'I've sent for you,' he told Swann, in his coldest voice, 'because I'm not satisfied with your conduct.' Then he turned, immediately and abruptly, to the Chief Steward. 'Let me have a report on this man.'

'Well, sir,' began Bryce, not sure what was expected of him, 'he's been generally slack and unreliable. He doesn't seem to – '

The Captain shook his head. 'No, no. Today. Tell me what he's been doing today.' Carefully he did not look at Swann; if possible, he wanted to isolate him, a small pocket of infection in a good clean ship. 'So far, I know that he went ashore without permission, and that he was logged when he came back. What happened then?'

Bryce, given the lead, went to work with a will. 'He disobeyed an order to report to me when he returned on board. He was logged for being absent without leave, within two hours of sailing time. He was reprimanded for not reporting, and reprimanded again for being found in a female passenger's cabin, which was not part of his section. He was reported for inattention and insolence by another passenger, Mr Ogilvie, B19, and reprimanded for the fourth time. When he became abusive, he was brought before the Staff Commander, taken off the passenger roster, and put to work in the junior officers' mess. He was insolent to the Staff Commander, and then went off to hold a stewards' meeting in the catering mess. He was brought out of that meeting, on your orders. His last words before he left were: "Don't worry, lads. I'll be back." On the way here, he had to be restrained by the Master-at-Arms, and he said something to me which I shall report to the Staff Commander.'

'What was that, Bryce?'

The Chief Steward cleared his throat. 'He said: "Why don't you join the bloody Gestapo? They could use a man like you." '

There was silence after Bryce's recital; a doubtful, waiting silence. Finally it was broken by a single dry sound from the direction of the porthole. Lord Calderstone, having struck a match, was lighting another cigar.

The Captain turned slightly to look at Swann. He found him as he expected to find him; gazing straight ahead, absolutely expressionless, holding himself apart from this particular bit of nonsense. They always behaved like this, the Captain thought; like kids who hid their eyes when the lightning started to play. If they pretended not to notice, everything would go away ... He tapped a pencil sharply on the desk, by way of a call to order, and when Swann looked towards the sound, he said: 'You're getting to be quite a problem, aren't you?'

Swann said nothing. He continued to look in the general direction of the Captain, but he made no further concession to brutal reality. After waiting a moment, the Captain asked: 'Well, what about it?'

Swann gave a start, as if suddenly recalled from dreamland. 'Oh,' he said, and then: 'Excuse me ... Is it all right for me to speak now?'

The Captain's mouth tightened; it was all the importance he allowed this minor piece of impudence. 'Yes, you can speak now. In fact I'm waiting. You've heard the Chief Steward's report on you. What have you got to say about it?'

'It's not all true,' said Swann.

'You mean, the Chief Steward is lying?'

'I mean, he's got his own point of view.'

'We all have,' said the Captain. 'And thank God for it. What's so different about Mr Bryce's point of view?'

'He's always on at me. He never leaves me alone. And it's not just me, either. He's chasing all of us up, all the time.'

'I'm glad to hear it,' said the Captain. 'It's known as maintaining discipline. It's his job, and he'd be a fool not to keep at it. What else?'

'He doesn't have to use threats and abuse,' said Swann virtuously. 'F'rinstance, he called me a bloody nuisance this afternoon.'

The Captain looked at him. 'We all get carried away sometimes ... Are you a bloody nuisance?'

'Of course not.'

'That's all right, then,' said the Captain, with marginal logic. 'No bones broken. *You* said he belonged to the Gestapo, and that's not true either.' His tone altered suddenly. 'Now let's hear about this meeting.'

With the change of tone, which he had not meant to sound so sharp, a change seemed to come over the room. It was as if some brief preliminary bout was over, without bloodshed, without decision; and now the gong was sounding for the main event, and that could be the one they had paid their money to see. Swann himself seemed suddenly to come to attention; his don't-care attitude, a stock tool on any occasion of discipline, firmed up subtly into caution. Even Lord Calderstone, drawing gently at his cigar on the outer rim of the cabin, became one of them again – a spectator whose attention is at last caught by something worth watching.

When Swann did not reply immediately, the Captain said sharply: 'Come on! I asked you a question. Let's hear the answer. You were at a meeting when the Chief Steward brought you out.'

'I was holding a meeting,' Swann corrected. 'A protest meeting.'

'How many were there?'

'About four hundred.'

If the figure were true, the Captain could not draw much comfort from it. Four hundred was well over half the catering staff. 'What was this protest about?'

Swann reacted to the curt tone. 'I've got a right to hold a meeting, if I want to. There's nothing in the regulations – '

'That's quite true,' the Captain interrupted. 'Though it's not usually such a good idea, just before sailing time, when most of the men attending it should be looking after their passengers … That wasn't what I asked you, in any case. What was the protest meeting about?'

Swann shrugged. 'All sorts of things. We've got grievances to discuss. We wanted to get them settled before we sailed.'

'What grievances?'

Swann jerked his head back towards Bryce. 'Him, for a start.'

'*Steward!*' said the Captain, so loudly and suddenly that everyone jumped.

'Yes, sir?' said Swann automatically.

'I was just going to point out that you haven't said "sir" to me since you came into my cabin. Now that you've started, just keep it up.'

'Yes, sir.'

'And when you're talking about the Chief Steward, call him Mr Bryce.'

'Yes, sir.'

'Very well.' In spite of Swann's subdued tone, the Captain knew that this was not real progress; a small improvement in attitude was not going to change anything important. All it had done was to restore his own sense of the fitness of things, and in the long run, or the short for that matter, that wasn't going to get them anywhere either. But he tried to press the small advantage. 'Now tell me about these so-called grievances.'

Swann was not put out by the phrase 'so-called'; for him, his grievances were real, floating vividly before his eyes, and he took the floor, and began to reel them off, with a readiness which more than anything else made the Captain suspect that they might not get very far with this interview. They were passing the time; and the time was passing them ... Swann's voice had become a sing-song recital, as if he were repeating a fairly recent speech.

'First of all we object to the way Bryce – Mr Bryce – pushes us about. We don't like the accommodation – there's too many men to one cabin. The food's not up to the standard laid down in the regulations, and when complaints are made, the man that complains is always victimized. We don't like the hours, particularly having to be on call so late at night. We want better recreation facilities, including the use of the swimming pool in off hours. We don't like the way the tips are carved up – the older chaps in the first class get all the best pickings.' His voice was growing stronger as he progressed. 'We've got our rights, same as other people, and we intend to see they're recognized. The mass demonstration tonight proves – ' He suddenly broke off, as if he had come out of a trance. 'That's about it,' he said carelessly. 'We're fed up with the way we're treated, and we're going to do something about it.'

Without giving him time to pause, the Captain asked: 'Where do you get all these ideas from?'

'I don't get them from anywhere,' said Swann perkily. 'It's just the way I feel. And most of the lads feel the same.'

'Then why hasn't the union brought up all these complaints, formally?'

'They have, some of them. Didn't get any joy. Seems like they need a bit more ginger.'

'Is that what the meeting was about?'

'Partly. And partly because of what the Staff Commander did to me.'

'What was that?'

'Took me off the Tourist roster, and put me with the officers.'

'What's wrong with that? You had it coming to you, Swann, and you know it. The Staff Commander had plenty of reason to discipline you, hadn't he?'

'That's his story,' said Swann, and added 'sir', for no reason that the Captain could divine. 'I was being victimized, that's all. And it was unconstitutional.' Good God, thought the Captain: where are we getting to now? 'Once the roster's made out for the voyage, it can't be changed. If I'm with the Tourist section, that's where I stay, no matter what happens.'

'Who says so?'

'It's the custom.'

The Captain glanced towards Bryce. 'True?'

'No, sir,' said Bryce stoutly. 'A man can be swapped round any time. Suppose there's only twenty first class, and a last minute rush of a hundred tourist class. It stands to reason we would have to – '

'All right,' said the Captain. 'I get it.' He turned back to Swann. 'You see? That isn't a proper grievance at all.'

'Well, we want that changed, too.'

The Captain looked at him. 'You want a lot of things changed, don't you? Or you pretend to. Now let's see if we can work out what it is you really want. First of all, you want to get out of here, and go back to your meeting. Right?

'Yes, sir,' said Swann, rather surprised.

'And then you want to play up this last grievance, and lead the men off.'

'There'll be a vote taken,' said Swann. 'It's all democratic, like. If there's a majority, we'll walk off. We're entitled to.'

'Are you so sure about that?'

Swann said: 'I'm sure of half the men, if that's what you mean. Better than half. They'll follow me. They don't follow anyone else.'

'I mean, are you so sure you're entitled to this walkout? When we've been delayed twenty-four hours already? When we're so close to sailing?'

'Right's right,' said Swann firmly. 'We've got these grievances, and they're going to be put straight. Otherwise' – he shrugged, the firm yet helpless shrug of a man caught up in great events – 'it's just another insult to the movement, and we're justified in taking strike action.'

There was a longer pause now, and for the Captain it began to hold elements of desperation. Swann's last words had made it clearer than ever that nothing was really happening; they were still getting nowhere; while they all pulled different ways, the *Good Hope* stayed firmly tied to the dock. Blacklock was now conscious, as never before on that day, of the fatal passage of time; time which was draining away their chances, lowering the tide level foot by foot, locking them in for the night. He wanted to make this point, loudly and indignantly, yet he could not do so; it would mean only good news for Swann, it would stiffen his skinny little backbone and make him more determined than ever to hold out ... Only one fact had so far emerged; they were getting nowhere, and it was twenty minutes past five.

Strangely, it was the Chief Steward who brought up this element of time; and he did so in an oddly heartening way, a way which gave a touch of bizarre sanity to the scene in the cabin. He had broken the silence by a discreet cough; now he said: 'Excuse me, sir. If there's nothing more for me to do, I'd like to get back to the dining room. I have to see about the seating for dinner.'

The Captain almost thanked him; Bryce's tone had been so normal, so matter-of-fact, letting it be known that in spite of all the uproar, he was thinking of this as just another voyage, and would be dealing with the machinery of departure just as he had done a hundred times before. Thank God for some solid men on board ... He answered: 'That's all right, Bryce. You carry on. I don't want to take up your time.'

'Will you eat on the bridge, sir?'

'Just some soup. I'll have a sandwich later.'

'Very good, sir. Er – have you finished with Swann?'

'No,' said the Captain. 'No, I have not.'

The Chief Steward must have had many other questions queuing up in his head, but he asked none of them. Instead, he gave a respectful nod in the direction of Lord Calderstone, turned smartly on his heel, and left the cabin.

The Captain looked at Swann, the isolated man he had not finished with. He said mildly: 'The Chief Steward seems to think we're sailing.'

Swann had not been daunted by isolation. It might be that he preferred it that way – the standard-bearer of unsullied democratic purity, assailed by dark, anti-social forces. He now produced a passable air of injury.

'I'm sure I don't know where he got that idea ... Can I go now, sir?'

'No,' said the Captain, 'I want to talk to you. In fact, I want to talk to you very seriously. Let's call it man to man. Without any witnesses.'

Swann glanced towards Lord Calderstone, that non-participating witness who, in silence or in full flood, was always there. *What about him?* his glance seemed to say. But he could not quite bring himself to phrase it so baldly, and he settled for an oblique objection. 'It depends what you call a witness, sir,'

'Lord Calderstone is Chairman of the line,' said the Captain coldly. 'He is at least as interested in this ship sailing as anyone on board. But he is not a witness in the sense you mean.' Abandoning ground which was not too tenable, the Captain hurried on. 'From what you've said, it sounds as if you think you can stop us sailing. Is that what you have in mind?'

Swann stuck to safer generalization. 'Like I said, we've got grievances. We want them put right, before we come to a settlement.'

'Even if that means we don't get away today?'

'Getting things put right is more important.'

The Captain went as far as he could bear to, on the road of cajolement. 'How about leaving things as they are now, and talking them over later?'

'It wouldn't work,' said Swann.

'Why not?'

'We've had enough of being fooled by the bosses.' He was setting out, at last, an intelligible statement of faith. 'Every time, they say, like, leave it for now, we'll talk about it later. But what happens? Nothing! We've just been led up the garden again. Well, it's gone on long enough.'

The Captain also had his faith, and it emerged suddenly in a burst of irritation.

'Good God, you talk as if we were starving you to death, grinding you into the gutter or something! Let me tell you, some of you chaps are damned lucky to have a job at all, the way you carry on! And if you do carry on like this, there won't be any sailing, and there won't be any jobs left.' In spite of himself, his eyes wandered to the clock, the enemy which was far stronger than Swann, and a hundred like him. 'Suppose – just suppose – that I keep you up here till it's past sailing time.'

Swann had his answer ready. 'We've got to sail by six o'clock, haven't we?'

'What of it?'

'The lads are waiting to hear from me. If I don't come down, they'll walk off anyway.' He had one more shot in his planned armoury, and he loosed it off with smug assurance. 'And if the gangways are taken off, there'll be a sit-down till we get to New York.'

It was the lowest point of all, the point when there really seemed no more hope. It was the point when the Captain, sitting behind his desk, found himself actually hating Swann for what he was doing to the ship, and to all the passengers and all their plans; the point when Swann, meeting his eyes boldly, could not repress a slight grin. It was the point when everything promising seemed to have come to an end, and the heartbeat of the *Good Hope*, which had been reaching the lively peak of departure, began imperceptibly to falter and to run down. It was the point when there seemed no prospect of anything save the dreary, shameful business of cancelling out.

It was the point at which Lord Calderstone suddenly moved in.

At one moment he had been in the shadows of the cabin, a tall man exhaling cigar smoke with detached pleasure; at the next, he had strode forward, and was standing over Swann – six feet two of formidable elegance confronting five feet six of nothing much. The Captain himself rose, involuntarily, and moved from behind his desk to a better vantage point. He could not guess what this strange collision of opposites might bring; but in case of crisis he was, without doubt, the only available referee.

Lord Calderstone started where the conversation had left off. 'The fact is, you are determined to stop this ship at all costs.'

Swann swallowed. It was not the sort of moment he had ever faced before, but he did his best.

'That's about it,' he said. 'If we don't get our rights.'

'Do you realize that, in that case, it is an illegal conspiracy in restraint of trade?'

'It's a walkout,' said Swann. 'Till we get our rights.'

'Rights!' echoed Lord Calderstone witheringly. 'You have a perfectly good union to look after your *rights*, as you call them, and it has operated perfectly satisfactorily until now. What conceivable authority have you, to try to usurp its functions? And what makes you think you can do any better by agitation? – by organizing an illegal strike just before we are due to sail?'

'We can always try,' said Swann, picking out the easy part of the question. He was gaining confidence, and with it came a quick flood of resentment. This old man was nothing to get alarmed about; there was just a lot of him, with a lot of fancy airs, and a lot of wind inside. And whatever he was, he had no right to come crowding in, poking his big nose into union business. 'We'll give it a fair shake, and see how it works out, eh?'

Lord Calderstone stared down at him. 'Do you know who I am?'

'The boss,' answered Swann. 'Lord Calderstone.' He produced a stage simper which tailed off into a sneer. 'Not that we've been introduced, of course. Excuse me for living, won't you?'

'I am the Chairman of Hope Lines,' said Lord Calderstone. Ignoring all impudence, he was speaking with a deliberate, cliff-like superiority which the Captain had never heard matched. 'This is one of our ships. She is due to sail in half an hour. Her punctuality is vital, for all sorts of reasons which I doubt if you could comprehend. Do you think I am going to permit hundreds of people to be inconvenienced, and thousands of pounds lost, because someone like you wants to have a last-minute argument about his rights?'

Swann, smarting under the tone, reacted snappishly. 'There's not much you can do about it, is there?'

'Don't be impertinent!'

'Well, don't push me about, then. I don't have to swallow this sort of talk, and say nothing in return. You're just taking a liberty, that's all it is! There's nothing that says I've got to put up with liberties, and I'm not going to!'

He was clearly near the end of his patience. Careless of discipline, he now moved to make his escape towards the door, but Lord Calderstone stood immovably in his way. The Captain stepped forward.

'Stop where you are,' he ordered. 'Lord Calderstone hasn't finished.'

'I've finished with him,' said Swann angrily. 'I don't have to stay here and listen to a lot of insults. Talking to me like I was dirt ... Those days are over, even if a lot of people haven't woken up to it yet.'

'You will stay here,' said Lord Calderstone bleakly, 'until I have told you exactly what I think of you. People like you, with your half-baked ideas and wildcat strikes and complete lack of responsibility, are the curse of this country, and it's time you took a good look at yourself. That is, if you have a strong enough stomach.'

Swann's face was mutinous. 'You can say what you like. It doesn't hurt me. Just sticks and stones ... What we want is a fair day's pay for a fair day's work. And we're going to get it!'

'I very much doubt if you have ever done a fair day's work in your life.'

'That's libel!' said Swann shrilly.

'Slander,' said Lord Calderstone. He surveyed Swann with a frosty aristocracy. 'And it gave me great pleasure. When *have* you done an ungrudging day's work? It's quite obvious that you people are determined to impose your own brand of social contract, which is to give the very minimum, and demand the maximum amount of money in return. There's only one word for you and your kind, Swann. You're a born loafer.'

Swann was standing absolutely still, between the enemy walls of Lord Calderstone and the Captain. He was biting his lip, controlling himself with an effort.

'You'll find out whether I'm a loafer or not,' he said venomously. 'I'm good enough to stop this ship any road. And I'm going to do it.'

'You couldn't stop a runaway roller skate,' said Lord Calderstone. For the first time, the Captain began to wonder at this ready flow of insult. Lord Calderstone could hardly have rehearsed the interview, but his words, his answering darts, were flying through the air so freely that they might have been part of a planned assault. If that were so, how was it meant to end, and in whose favour? ... Lord Calderstone was continuing, on the same note of absolute contempt: 'You're only a mouthpiece for that disgusting fellow ashore, in any case. McTeague ... He whistles the tune, and you have to go through your wretched little dance. That's not a man's job, Swann. It's more of a girl's. But you were given a man's name, weren't you?'

'That's provocation!' shouted Swann – and the Captain was now sure that it was, as swift and as crude as Lord Calderstone could make it. 'I won't stay here to listen to this! Let me go!'

'You have a real man's name,' said Lord Calderstone, as if he had not heard a word. 'I took the trouble to acquaint myself with it, while you were being brought up here. Victor Winston Swann. Victor Winston.' His tone had grown murderously sarcastic. 'Do you know what it used to stand for, in the days when your mother and father chose it? Do you know what it still stands for? "Victor" for the will to work and fight, and "Winston" for the greatest Englishman of this century. He was almost bending over Swann, staring down at him as if he were some horrible mess on the floor. 'And they had to go and tack it on to you ... You and your family should be arrested for false pretences, for public insult ... If I were concerned with your christening, which God forbid, do you know what I should do? I wouldn't trouble to find a name for you. I should drown you in the font.'

The Captain knew, a moment before it happened, that Swann was going to lunge towards the door, and that he would get there at all costs; his clenched fists and trembling body could only belong to a man taunted and provoked beyond endurance. Moved by common prudence, Blacklock stepped forward, intent on bringing things under control again; and as he did so, it happened.

Swann shouted: 'Let me go! Get out of my road!' and raised both fists, prepared to push his tormentor from his path. Then he took a pace forward, and shoved furiously, with all his might. The Captain, moving in front of Lord Calderstone, became the actual, inevitable target.

The blow, vicious rather than heavy, caught Blacklock full in the face, between cheekbone and jaw. As he fell back, startled and stung, he blinked his eyes shut; and when he opened them again, they had all of them fallen back, shunning the trap of nearness, and a terrible silence settled over the cabin.

It was ended at last by the luckless man who had made it. Swann's pale face was sweating; he was looking anywhere except at the Captain – at the floor, at the lamp on the desk, at the smarting knuckles of his hand, which had so appallingly betrayed him. Trouble loomed over his head like a wave, about to break in a roaring flurry.

'Sorry, sir,' he muttered, utterly shame-faced. 'I didn't mean – '

The Captain, hand still to his cheek, took him up, in a voice grimly furious. 'You didn't mean *what*?'

'To do that.'

Swann's glance was now fixed miserably on his feet.

'Look at me!' said the Captain. 'You damned little tyke! You didn't mean to do *what*?'

'To give you a push, like.'

'You didn't push me, you hit me.'

'It was an accident.'

'It was nothing of the sort! You meant to land a blow, and you did. Do you know what the penalty is for striking an officer?'

'I didn't strike you, sir.'

Lord Calderstone made a small, silky contribution. 'It was my impression that you did.'

Swann looked from one to the other; from Lord Calderstone, the most formidable witness there could ever be, to the Captain, standing there with the mark already reddening on his cheek – the unarguable mark, plain for all to see, the damning evidence of assault. He had been trapped in deep trouble, and he knew it.

The Captain confirmed it. 'You lost your temper and you hit me. I have a witness to that.' At long last, in all this mess, he had glimpsed his chance, and he made to seize it. 'Once again, do you know what the penalty is for striking an officer?'

'No, sir.'

'It can be prison,' said the Captain. 'Trial ashore, and a prison sentence.'

Swann made one last brave effort. 'Better put me ashore then, sir.'

'I will not put you ashore,' said the Captain. He had walked back to his desk, and sat down again. 'This ship is under sailing orders, and no one is going ashore. You will make the trip across the Atlantic in the brig, you will be shipped back from New York the same way, and you will be charged here in Liverpool when you get back, about three weeks from now.'

'He provoked me.' Swann, still struggling feebly, indicated Lord Calderstone. 'Why should I sit down when there's provocation?'

The Captain returned Lord Calderstone's compliment. 'I didn't hear any provocation. I heard a lot of clap-trap about rights and fair play, and then you lost your temper, and broke out.'

'Why shouldn't we fight to get fair play?' Swann tried to shift his ground, somewhere safer, anywhere. 'We're human beings. It's the class struggle. And the public's behind us.'

'Don't fool yourself,' said the Captain roughly. 'The public's sick and tired of the whole lot of you. And so am I.' He paused, collecting himself for the last effort. 'You've been telling me a lot of things in the past half hour. Now I'll tell you some.' He had to look round his desk, which was newly arranged for him, before he came up with what he wanted – a copy of *Cole's Merchant Shipping Acts,* and a stack of printed forms. He turned back to Swann again. 'Do you remember the Articles of Agreement you signed when you shipped aboard the *Good Hope*?'

'Yes, sir,' said Swann forlornly. He didn't remember them; in fact he had never read them; he only knew what they could do.

'You signed them, of your own free will,' said the Captain. 'They're a contract – not between you and the company, but between you and me. They cover a lot of things. Over the last hundred years, they've tried to cover everything. I'll tell you two of the things they certainly do cover.'

Without hurrying, however much he wanted to, he ran his thumb down the Articles of Agreement; then he opened *Cole's,* looked up a passage, and shut the book with a resounding bang. He was ready.

'Part of that personal contract you made with me takes care of two things – discipline and violence; and it sets out the penalties – what happens to you if you break your word. First, there's the offence known as disobedience of any lawful command. There's a scale of fines that goes with that.' He looked, without favour, at Swann. 'I reckon you know that already.'

'Yes, sir.'

'By God, you ought to! ... Then there's a clause that makes it an offence' – he glanced down, to read the passage – 'to strike or assault any person on board or belonging to the ship. Penalty for that, a fine equal to one day's pay for the first occasion, two days' pay for the second. If not otherwise prosecuted.'

'Yes, sir.' Swann's dejected expression showed sudden signs of life. This might not be so bad after all. The bit about prison now sounded like some sort of try-on. A fine wasn't going to trouble him. Mostly the union paid them, anyway. And he'd still be able to –

'*If not otherwise prosecuted!*' said the Captain, almost at the top of his voice. He had seen the look on Swann's face, and he intended to change it, perhaps forever. 'In both those cases, I have the option of imposing a fine, after a full inquiry on board, or of sending you ashore to be prosecuted.'

Swann waited. The Captain took a last glance at the Articles of Agreement.

'At my discretion,' he said, 'instead of being dealt with by me, you can be taken before a summary court ashore, and prosecuted under Section 225 of the Merchant Shipping Act. The Act lays down the penalties, so you know what you're in for before you start.' He read them out, with a rolling relish. 'They are: for wilful disobedience of a lawful command, imprisonment for four weeks, and forfeiture of two days' wages. For assault of the Master, or any mate, or any certified engineer; imprisonment for twelve weeks.'

Swann drew in his breath sharply; on his shocked face, the echo of 'imprisonment for twelve weeks' seemed to be printed already, the crushing price tag of failure. It was the end of the road. He looked at Lord Calderstone, and Lord Calderstone stared back at him like the implacable image of justice; he looked at the Captain, and with all deliberation the Captain spoke.

'Circumstances can alter cases. That is why I am given that discretion. I can settle this on board, with a fine, or I can send you ashore to a magistrate's court. There you would get up to three months in jail. As far as I'm concerned, you deserve it, every time. But if possible, I want to save myself the trouble. I want to save myself *any* trouble. You understand?'

'Yes, sir.'

He understood, well enough. He was being offered a bargain, and it was a bargain he would have to accept, whether he liked it or not; between them, they had carved him up. He remembered McTeague's parting words: 'Any fool can go to jail.' For what he had done, he could be sent to jail. It wasn't his fault, but that wouldn't show on the record. He could be sent to jail, and thereafter be written off as a fool. He had made a mess of this one, a real dog's dinner. There would be a next time, and a time after that. But this time, he had lost.

The Captain looked at the clock. It was twenty-five minutes to six. He cleared his throat.

'I'm glad you understand,' he said. 'I don't want anything to go wrong at the last minute ... Now just you listen to me. In accordance with that personal contract we both signed, I will now give you a lawful command. Go below, put on your proper rig, and get back to your duties.'

There would be a next time, thought Swann. He'd tell the lads that, as soon as he could get them together. But this time . . .

'Yes, sir,' he said, and turned, and walked quietly out.

She had passed the Bar Light Vessel, fourteen miles down river, with ten minutes to spare; and now, as the solitary light blinked and faded far astern, the *Good Hope* began to stir and to lift. A small wave broke under her forefoot, and then another; a drift of spray landed on the foc's'le-head, and spread till it was picked up by the rising moon, and glittered like scattered jewellery. The massive hull started its endless creaking. She was at sea.

The Captain stood on the wing of the bridge, slowly shedding some of his cares. The pilot had been dropped, the Third Officer had the watch; moving into deep water, winning her searoom, the *Good Hope* was less of a burden and more of a prize. Even when Lord Calderstone joined him – and he was the only passenger who could conceivably have been allowed to do so – he did not mind.

Lord Calderstone was in fine and mellow spirits. The drift of cigar smoke, the discreet waft of brandy, testified to an after-dinner relaxation. He leant against the bridge rail, and, like the Captain, stared at the horizon ahead, the margin of inky sea which suddenly became the paler sky. He looked benignly at the moon, he glanced at the Great Bear and the Pole Star; they might have all been in his family for several generations. Then he said, as if there had been no three-hour interval: 'He had a weak point. Among his many weak points. Bad temper. I noticed it when Bryce was making his report. Swann was pretending not to listen, but he was sucking his teeth all the time. People of that class do not suck their teeth unless they are seriously concerned.'

The Captain had had enough surprises and alarms for that day, and he took this one in his stride. 'You did it on purpose, then? You were working on him.'

'Oh yes.' Lord Calderstone's cigar glowed brightly. 'I did not know what would happen, but I knew that something would. He was that sort of customer. It was intolerably crude, of course, but time was getting short.' The cigar glowed again. 'By the way, I thought you handled it extremely well.'

The words, which should have been balm for any new captain, were not as welcome as they might have been, and in the darkness Blacklock found himself frowning. The Swann episode had left a decided taste. Not a bad taste, because their side had won. But not a good taste, either. It had all been so damned crude, as the Chairman had said. One-sided, in numbers and in authority. Bullying. Cooked up. Unscrupulous. Rather unfair.

As if picking up his thought, Lord Calderstone went on: 'We had to do it like that, don't you agree? After all, they were going to do it to us. In the circumstances, it seemed that any weapons were excusable, even the most barbarous. I simply used what came to hand.'

Maybe that was the answer, or part of it; enough for the voyage, anyway.

Lord Calderstone added, in what must have been a rare phrase: 'Anyway, I was very glad to be of help.'

The night was growing colder. The Captain settled his neck deeper into the collar of his bridge coat, and still stared ahead. All round him, his ship, ploughing a long silvery furrow across the Irish Sea, was solid and secure. But he was still not quite at ease. The *Good Hope* had sailed, in spite of all tricks to the contrary, and maybe that was enough, for this day, for this voyage. But it really would not do for a solid future.

Lord Calderstone, aware of silence, glanced sideways at the man he could just see in the starlight. He was still jovial in victory, but he sought to express it benevolently, discerningly.

'I expect you think this is a perfectly terrible way to run a ship.'

The Captain expelled a long breath. He had his private thoughts, and up on his own bridge he could put them any way he chose, even to the Chairman. Especially on a night like this. He said: 'I think it's a hell of a way to run anything.'

Nicholas Monsarrat

The Pillow Fight

Passion, conflict and infidelity are vividly depicted in this gripping tale of two people and their marriage. Set against the glittering background of glamorous high life in South Africa, New York and Barbados, an idealistic young writer tastes the corrupting fruits of success, while his beautiful, ambitious wife begins to doubt her former values. A complete reversal of their opposing beliefs forms the bedrock of unremitting conflict. Can their passion survive the coming storm …?

'Immensely readable … an eminently satisfying book'
Irish Times

'A professional who gives us our money's worth. The entertainment value is high'
Daily Telegraph

Smith and Jones

Within the precarious conditions of the Cold War, diplomats Smith and Jones are not to be trusted. But although their files demonstrate evidence of numerous indiscretions and drunkenness, they have friends in high places who ensure that this doesn't count against them, and they are sent across the Iron Curtain.

However, when they defect, the threat of absolute treachery means that immediate and effective action has to be taken. At all costs and by whatever means, Smith and Jones must be silenced.

'An exciting and intriguing story'
Daily Express

'In this fast-moving Secret Service story Nicholas Monsarrat has brought off a neat tour de force with a moral'
Yorkshire Post

NICHOLAS MONSARRAT

THIS IS THE SCHOOLROOM

The turbulent Thirties, and all across Europe cry the discordant voices of hunger and death, most notably in Spain, where a civil war threatens to destroy the country.

Aspiring writer, Marcus Hendrycks, has toyed with life for twenty-one years. His illusions, developed within a safe, cloistered existence in Cambridge, are shattered forever when he joins the fight against the fascists and is exposed to a harsh reality. As the war takes hold, he discovers that life itself is the real schoolroom.

'... the quintessential novel of its time and an indictment of an age, stands today as a modern classic'
Los Angeles Times

THE WHITE RAJAH

The breathtaking island of Makassang, in the Java Sea, is the setting for this tremendous historical novel. It is a place both splendid and savage, where piracy, plundering and barbarism are rife.

The ageing Rajah, threatened by native rebellion, enlists the help of Richard Marriott – baronet's son-turned-buccaneer – promising him a fortune to save his throne. But when Richard falls in love with the Rajah's beautiful daughter, the island, and its people, he find himself drawn into a personal quest to restore peace and prosperity.

'A fine swashbuckler by an accomplished storyteller'
New York Post

Nicholas Monsarrat

The Tribe That Lost Its Head

Five hundred miles off the southwest coast of Africa lies the island of Pharamaul, a British Protectorate, governed from Whitehall through a handful of devoted British civilians. In the south of the island lies Port Victoria, dominated by the Governor's palatial mansion; in the north, a settlement of mud huts shelter a hundred thousand natives; and in dense jungle live the notorious Maula tribe, kept under surveillance by a solitary District Officer and his young wife. When Chief-designate, Dinamaula, returns from his studies in England with a spirited desire to speed the development of his people, political crisis erupts into a ferment of intrigue and violence.

'A splendidly exciting story'
Sunday Times

Richer Than All His Tribe

The sequel to *The Tribe That Lost Its Head* is a compelling story which charts the steady drift of a young African nation towards bankruptcy, chaos and barbarism.

On the island of Pharamaul, a former British Protectorate, newly installed Prime Minister, Chief Dinamaula, celebrates Independence Day with his people, full of high hopes for the future.

But the heady euphoria fades and Dinamaula's ambitions and ideals start to buckle as his new found wealth corrupts him, leaving his nation to spiral towards hellish upheaval and tribal warfare.

'Not so much a novel, more a slab of dynamite'
Sunday Mirror

OTHER TITLES BY NICHOLAS MONSARRAT AVAILABLE DIRECT FROM HOUSE OF STRATUS

Quantity		£	$(US)	$(CAN)	€
☐	HMS Marlborough Will Enter Harbour	6.99	11.50	15.99	11.50
☐	Life is a Four-Letter Word	6.99	11.50	15.99	11.50
☐	The Master Mariner	6.99	11.50	15.99	11.50
☐	The Nylon Pirates	6.99	11.50	15.99	11.50
☐	The Pillow Fight	6.99	11.50	15.99	11.50
☐	Richer Than All His Tribe	6.99	11.50	15.99	11.50
☐	Smith and Jones	6.99	11.50	15.99	11.50
☐	Something to Hide	6.99	11.50	15.99	11.50
☐	The Story of Esther Costello	6.99	11.50	15.99	11.50
☐	This is the Schoolroom	6.99	11.50	15.99	11.50
☐	The Time Before This	6.99	11.50	15.99	11.50
☐	The Tribe That Lost Its Head	6.99	11.50	15.99	11.50
☐	The White Rajah	6.99	11.50	15.99	11.50

Please allow following postage costs per order:

	£(Sterling)	$(US)	$(CAN)	€(Euros)
UK	1.95	3.20	4.29	3.00
Europe	2.95	4.99	6.49	5.00
North America	2.95	4.99	6.49	5.00
Rest of World	2.95	5.99	7.75	6.00
Free carriage for goods value over:	50	75	100	75

PLEASE SEND CHEQUE, POSTAL ORDER (STERLING ONLY), EUROCHEQUE, OR INTERNATIONAL MONEY ORDER (PLEASE CIRCLE METHOD OF PAYMENT YOU WISH TO USE)

MAKE PAYABLE TO: STRATUS HOLDINGS plc

Order total including postage:______ Please tick currency you wish to use and add total amount of order:

☐ £ (Sterling) ☐ $ (US) ☐ $ (CAN) ☐ € (EUROS)

VISA, MASTERCARD, SWITCH, AMEX, SOLO, JCB:

☐☐☐☐☐☐☐☐☐☐☐☐☐☐☐☐☐☐☐☐

Issue number (Switch only):

☐☐☐

Start Date:

☐☐/☐☐

Expiry Date:

☐☐/☐☐

Signature: ____________________

NAME: ____________________

ADDRESS: ____________________

____

POSTCODE: ____________

Please allow 28 days for delivery.

Prices subject to change without notice.
Please tick box if you do not wish to receive any additional information. ☐